A Little Lipstick Wouldn't Hurt

An Unfriendly Welcome
Small Town Rom-Com

Indie Sparks

Twice Shy Publishing

Letting a man ruin
your lipstick is harmless.
Letting him ruin your
plans is out of the
question!

~ from the philosophy of
Glynnis Ramsey

1

Glynnis

I LEISURELY SPIN THE postcard rack at the front of the antique shop but stop it abruptly when my eyes land on a vintage card with a raven-haired pin-up girl. Lifting the faded-around-the-edges card, I smile at her red lipstick.

Her blue and white polka dot swimsuit is adorable. The canary yellow scarf tied in her dark hair is the perfect compliment. They weren't afraid of color back then, that's for sure.

Things weren't so matchy-matchy in pin-up style, and I abso-fuckinglutely love it.

This card was meant to promote the model's red shoes, but those lips . . . it's so hard to convince women it's okay to wear red lipstick these days. Women back then didn't get lip injections, but they all looked good with a red lip.

"Victory Red," I mutter to no one.

Women still look amazing in red lipstick; they just need the right red for them. Every woman should have a signature red in her arsenal. Red is revolutionary.

And women should wake up ready to revolt every goddamn day.

Speaking of red, I look out the window to make sure I don't miss the pickup truck I'm expecting. Grinberry Falls is growing, but the locals still schedule meetings in general timeframes. I have a meeting at "ten or so."

Does that mean ten, ten-fifteen, ten-thirty? Hell if I know. I've visited my best friend multiple times since she moved here, but I'm definitely not fluent in small-town Texan.

A familiar warmth skates up the back of my neck, tickling my ear and the backs of my knees at the same time. His voice stimulates as much as it startles—a baritone vibration flowing over my skin like warm honey, dripping with dominance instead of sweetness.

"Hey, Twister. I thought you weren't getting in until tonight."

The postcard bends in my hand as I fight not to clench my fist. My entire core has already clenched on instinct. With a deep breath, I slip the card back into the rack and turn to face him.

"I came in early for a meeting."

Damn, the way my fingers itch to unsnap his shirt. I can already hear the zipper-like sound of those pearl snaps popping. My eyes follow them all the way down to his belt buckle before I'm able to yank them back up again.

His smile is wolfish, just the way I like it.

"Where'd you come from?" I ask.

"I was in the back, dropping off some stickers so Kay can re-stock."

"She sells stickers for the recording studio?"

"Yep. Talking about t-shirts next." He shakes his head. "Never thought I'd see the day."

"Face it, you're an icon."

"Right. You've got a meeting, huh? In Grinberry Falls?"

"I do. I'm meeting with Huck James. He owns the little blue house next to Trudy's Diner."

"I'm familiar with Huck and his real estate assets." His eyebrows arch with suspicion. "He's also on the Keep Grinberry Falls Local committee. You know, the one that ensures Main Street businesses are owned and operated by locals."

"Of course, he is. You've strong-armed every business owner in town to join your exclusive little committee." I can't resist reaching a fingertip to trace the stitching on the button placket running down his chest. "But as I recall, the committee's goal is to have ninety-percent local ownership on Main Street, not to shut out newcomers entirely. Anyway, how do you know I'm not inquiring about the cute little blue house because I'd like to have a place in town to stay when I visit Sabrina?"

"Sabrina and Mav have a guest cabin. And two extra bedrooms in their house. You already have a place to stay. Besides, Huck's little blue house is commercially zoned."

He captures my wrist and brings it to his mouth. His kiss is soft, but his grip is firm.

"Fine. You found me out. I'm bringing Sugar Lips to Main Street." My voice only wavers the tiniest bit at the end when he tightens his fingers around my wrist.

"Why not open a location of your lip spa in the new shopping center out by the highway?"

"That's not even in Grinberry Falls. I have reasons for wanting my store to be on Main Street."

"And I have reasons to keep that from happening." He releases my wrist with a smile, as if he's not being totally confrontational for no reason other than his own damn stubbornness.

Huck's fire-engine red pickup truck (his definition, not mine) drives past. He parks in front of the diner.

"Well, gotta go. It looks like my meeting's about to start."

"You're wasting your time. Meet me at Grin's after you're done."

"Sure thing . . . *Daddy*." I let a fingertip slip between his buttons as I whisper the title. His abs contract, and his gaze goes steely. A glance at his crotch lets me know I've imbued a little steel there, too. Good. Turnabout's fair play.

"I'll text you when I head that way," I say with a smile. "Have an espresso martini ready and waiting for me so we can celebrate my soon-to-be fourth location."

"You'll need that martini to console yourself after Huck refuses to rent the space to you."

"Yeah, I don't see that happening."

I stride out the door, letting it sweep closed behind me. The tinkling sound of the bells swinging against the paint-chipped wood lingers in my ears as I walk. I've got this. And if it's more difficult than I'm anticipating, I'm not above turning on the charm to get what I want.

Though admittedly, I'm not accustomed to using my charms on one man while my panties are wet from the influence of another.

Goddamn, you, Rhett Wilding.

2
Rhett

I SWEAR, GLYNNIS RAMSEY knocks me off kilter quicker than the damn flu. It's not an unfair comparison either. She comes on strong out of nowhere, then leaves me disoriented and feverish. God knows the symptoms are a hell of a lot more enjoyable when she causes them, though.

"Hey, Kay!" I call out loud enough for her to hear in her office. "How much are these postcards?"

"For you? No charge!" she yells back. "Unless you want the whole damn rack."

"Nah, just this one." I hold it up so Kay can see it because she's poked her head around the corner.

"She's a beauty. And all yours."

"Thanks." I appreciate the gesture, but it's not at all for me.

Mav looks up from wiping down the bar when I walk into Grin's Pub. He's the third-generation owner. None of us expected him to stay when he came back to town after his dad died, but this town's better off for having him here.

There was a time when I'd have said staying wasn't what was best for him, but then Sabrina came to town, and those two are meant for each other like no couple I've ever known.

Of course, if not for Sabrina, I'd have never met Glynnis, so as far as I'm concerned, we're all better off for having her in Grinberry Falls, too.

I claim a barstool. "I guess you already know Twister's in town."

He winces. "Yeah, I might've been vaguely aware of that blonde cyclone rolling up my driveway last night."

"She's been here since last night?"

"Sorry, man. I was sworn to secrecy. You drinking coffee or beer?"

"Beer, but only because it's too early for whiskey." I'm not much of a whiskey drinker these days, but Mav understands the point I'm making with the joke.

"So, you've seen her face-to-face then." His smile is friendly, but his tone leaves no doubt he's giving me shit for the way she affects me.

I'm not one to be easily rattled. Hell, I work with some of the biggest names in Nashville, and even those walking egos don't affect me.

But Glynnis is in a league of her own. The public answer to why I call her Twister is because she whips around like a tornado, switching direction without notice and leaving a path of devastation in her wake, but the private truth is that she twists me up emotionally like a fucking pretzel.

She's a strong, independent woman, but she takes direction incredibly well in certain moments. And when that woman calls me Daddy . . . fuck me. There is nothing I would deny her.

If she ever figures that out, she could own me.

We just sort of happened into a situation. Nothing exclusive, but no one else compares, so why would I bother with anyone else? Our kinks line up, sure, but there's a mutual respect behind it all, and having the whole package in one woman is hotter than asphalt in August.

I set the postcard I bought her on the bar and close my hand around the cold beer Mav's slid my way.

"What's that?" he asks, nodding at the pin-up girl in the fuck-me heels.

"It's for Twister. She was looking at it in Kay's shop when I surprised her from behind. I think she liked the shoes."

"Or maybe the lipstick?"

For such a cocky motherfucker, he does have good instincts when it comes to women. He's one of those guys who pays attention to details, and unlike those of us who can do so quietly, he's too much of a smartass not to showboat what he's noticed every now and then. Especially if he can use it to bust my balls.

In the case of this postcard, he's clearly seen what I missed. She owns a chain of lip spas, but I assumed she liked the postcard for the shoes because it's an ad for shoes. She'll probably frame it and hang it in one of her locations solely because of the red lips.

I may not have noticed the model's lipstick, but I never fail to pay attention to Glynnis's red lips, and I'm pretty sure that counts for a hell of a lot more.

This sexy postcard won't be hanging on Main Street, though.

I don't really have a choice in opposing her opening a location on Main Street. I founded the Keep Grinberry Falls Local committee. How would it look if I didn't challenge an outsider just because my dick twitches and my mouth waters with the memory of her taste the moment I lay eyes on her?

Just because she calls me . . . aw, shit, this is gonna get ugly.

I take a long swig from the perfectly poured beer in front of me.

My eyes drift to the door in time to see her approach through the glass. If I didn't know better, I'd say that's a victory smile on her gorgeous face.

Huck would never.

Who am I trying to kid? Like hell he wouldn't.

It's fine. Even if he crumpled like a damp dish rag, the committee will challenge it.

Let her have her fun. The committee's regulations are solid. Rules are rules.

3
Glynnis

THE TOWN'S UNOFFICIAL MASCOT, an alpaca named Oliver, prances down the sidewalk in front of me. Looks like he's headed for Grin's, too. I rush ahead to open the door for him.

For Oliver, Grin's is a literal watering hole. Mav keeps a sawed-off, five-gallon bucket behind the bar to give the alpaca water whenever he needs it.

Mav and Sabrina never even held a grudge against Oliver for trashing their wedding cake. This alpaca is revered in Grinberry Falls.

When I pull the door open, Oliver turns his head and pretends not to see me standing there. He steps away and refuses to look at me at all.

Oh, I get it. He wants to ring the doorbell. I'm stealing his thunder.

As preposterous as it sounds, it's true. Mav installed a doorbell so Oliver can buzz for service when he needs water. This beast is a total diva, which I lowkey respect, even as he's disrespecting me in the middle of the damn sidewalk.

I step inside and watch the door close, but I wait right there because I know Oliver is about to ring the doorbell. There's no need for Mav to step out from behind the bar and walk all the way over here just to open the door when I can easily wait and do it myself.

Oliver side-eyes me through the window. What is he waiting for now?

Oh, you have got to be kidding me. He's waiting for me to leave before he rings the bell?

I press my back to the wall between the door and the window, hoping he won't be able to see me there. Out of sight, out of mind, right? How smart can an alpaca be?

After standing there for what feels like five minutes, I concede that he might be smarter than I thought.

Fine. I give up.

The moment my ass meets my barstool, the doorbell chimes.

"Are you kidding me? He wouldn't let me open the door for him. He wouldn't even use the doorbell while I was standing there."

"It's fine," Mav says, passing me one of his world-class espresso martinis. "Enjoy your drink. I've got Oliver."

I blink at the bar top next to where Rhett's hand is resting. "You bought that?"

He nods and pushes the postcard closer to me. "Figured you might've been planning to do it before I surprised you. Only seemed fair to get it for you. Think of it as a consolation prize."

"Thank you." I slip the postcard into my purse. "You're right. I was thinking about buying it."

He smirks at me in my peripheral vision.

"What are you looking so smug about?" I take a sip of my drink as if I have no idea why he's feeling superior. Of course, I know exactly why he looks like he just played the final winning hand in a game of strip poker. But I also know something he doesn't know I know.

I pull my head back and nod approvingly at the rim of my glass. My no-smudge lip gloss lives up to its hype. Not a hint of a lip print to be found.

"I take it your meeting went well?" he muses.

"It did. How's your beer?"

"How's my beer? Really, Twister?"

"Well, I figured if we're asking silly questions, I should be a good sport and play along."

"While your good sportsmanship is appreciated, I'd actually like to hear about your meeting."

"Cool. What do you want to know?"

His jaw flexes. He's annoyed. He'd be even more annoyed if he knew how much I loved knowing I've gotten under his skin. Rhett doesn't like to be toyed with. That's too bad because I'm in the mood to play.

He'll survive it. Suffering builds character.

"So, when's the ribbon cutting ceremony?" He says it in the same condescending tone you'd use to wish a five-year-old safe travels after they tell you they're running away because you wouldn't let them have cookies for dinner.

Oh, he's toying with me now, huh? Little does he know . . .

"Well, first we have to get through the inspections and the appraisal. Then after the closing, I'll start the remodel. Of course, I'll have to get bids first, and I have no idea how long it takes to get a permit in this town. Do new businesses generally cut the ribbon at the beginning or the end of a build-out?"

His stare is blank, and I can't say I've ever seen that expression on him before.

"I guess I should know the answer to that," I go on, undeterred. "But I've never owned my own building before. My other three locations are all leased. I didn't come to Grinberry Falls to lease, though; I came to buy. Those ordinances your committee put into effect are ironclad when it comes to renting space to businesses not owned by locals."

I pause to take another sip of my drink before I officially ruin his morning.

"It turns out, however, that the covenants for keeping things local don't put any restrictions on who the property owners can sell to. Of course, real estate laws are pretty tricky when it comes to restricting who buyers can and cannot sell to, but you'd think a committee hellbent on keeping certain people out might have bothered to try. Anyway, it turns out there is actually no mention at all about where the owner of the business can be from if they also own the property. Only business owners who rent are restricted. Wild, huh?"

If his stare was blank before, he's completely left his body at this point.

I lift my glass. "Cheers! I'm buying the little blue house on Main Street. Can you believe it? Contract's all signed. I know how badly you want all the business owners downtown to join your committee, but I'll probably hold off on trying to assimilate with the locals. How long do you think it'll take before people around here start to consider me a local?"

"Well, first you'd have to move here, and we both know that's not happening. You're not leaving Scottsdale for Grinberry Falls, so why would you make an offer to buy property here? It's one thing to rent a building when you live somewhere else, Twister. The landlord is there to take care of any issues that come up. But when you're two states away, how the hell are you going to manage the place?"

"First of all, it's not an offer; it's a signed contract. Second of all, I'm buying it because you forced my hand. And third of all, lots of businesses buy property in states where the owners don't live. The home of the business owner has nothing to do with it. It's all about what makes sense for the business. And this makes sense for Sugar Lips."

"Nothing about this makes sense!"

Oliver's hooves clack against the old wooden floor planks as he walks away from his water bucket. Mav doesn't immediately follow him to the door, obviously waiting to see what I'll say next.

"My CPA disagrees." I take another sip of my drink. Mav really does make the best espresso martinis. "Oh, shit! I haven't even told Sabrina yet!"

"Was it your brilliant CPA who found the loophole in our guidelines?"

"Nope. I found it all by my little lonesome. Then my attorney confirmed it, my CPA gave the financial stamp of approval, and here we are."

"Here we are."

"Yep."

"Your team works fast," he says.

"Yeah, life in general moves a little faster outside the city limits of Grinberry Falls."

"So I've heard."

"Let me guess, you're rethinking not having a big-city attorney review those commercial CC&Rs right about now?" I know I'm poking the bear, but like I said, I'm in the mood to play.

"I'm thinking how good my big handprint would look on your pretty little ass right about now."

I down the rest of my drink in one gulp. "Oops, I think I drank too much to drive. I guess I need a ride."

"I'll give you the ride of your life, darlin'."

We both abandon our barstools and head for the door.

"Don't worry about the tab or anything," Mav calls after us.

"We'll settle up tomorrow," Rhett says. "She's got a more immediate debt to pay."

"That's funny," I say. "I was under the impression you owed me."

His voice is a low growl in my ear when he asks, "Do you want me to spank you right here?"

I purr my response. "Not today, Daddy. But never say never."

"Careful what you promise, Twister."

"Careful what you threaten."

We crash through the door and practically race to his truck. Oliver crosses in front of us as we wait to pull onto Main Street. He pauses to munch on some sunflowers growing in an old bathtub in front of the barber shop, and I smile as I watch him.

I may not be a small-town girl, but this place does have its quirky charms.

Rhett's strong hand squeezes my thigh. I don't even attempt to fight the clenching sensations that seize my core.

Most days, buying a house would be the most exciting thing that happened to me. It would overshadow anything that followed, but as soon as we get to his ranch, Rhett's extraordinary hands are going to make buying that house seem like the most ordinary thing in the world.

I could buy a house anywhere, any time. But when Rhett takes control, my whole world tilts on its axis.

Thank goddess he doesn't know he has that kind of power over me.

4

Rhett

T HE WIND KICKS UP as Glynnis hops down out of my truck, whipping the thick layers of her shoulder-length blonde hair around her face.

She blows right back as if the wind will bend to her will. I'm amazed that none of her hair sticks to her lip gloss, but I know from kissing her that it's shiny without being sticky. She calls it smudge-proof. I'm not entirely convinced it's not witchcraft.

That stuff could probably be patented as some sort of marine coating. Not that I'm going to suggest that to her. I'd never want her to think I was belittling her business by joking about it. God knows, I hear my share of bullshit about how I get paid for doing nothing. People are experts in their own mind on a whole lot of things they know fuck-all about.

She's proud of her products, as she should be. Her accomplishments are impressive.

I'll never admit it to her, but I'm even impressed at the way she outsmarted me when it comes to keeping Grinberry Falls local. That doesn't mean I won't try to nix her plans, but it reminds me why we're here.

I pin her to the closed door of my truck, my hips pressing into hers while my hands capture her wrists above her head. The wind assaults my back now, blowing her hair away from her face.

Jesus, she's beautiful. Her gray-blue eyes sparkle in the sunlight. They're a little glassy from watering in the wind, but she meets my stare with them held wide open. There's always a hint of a dare in those eyes. Except when the dare is all there is, like right now.

She's not daring me to make good on my intentions; she's daring me not to.

And I wouldn't dare let her down.

I can feel the fabric of her skirt twist as I grind against her, crushing my mouth on hers. She can wear the hell out of a pair of jeans, but when she's in a short little skirt like the one she's wearing right now, it's all I can do to peel my eyes off the hem. Or the switch of her ass just inches above it.

"Turn around and put your hands on the truck."

It's my turn to issue dares now.

My house is more than a mile from the road. The ranch is remote enough that the only watchful eyes are mine and those of my guests. And other than her, I don't currently have any guests.

The studio is on the property, too, but no one's recording today. It's too far from the house for anyone to accidentally see us, anyway.

It's just us and the wind.

She draws the corner of her lip between her teeth and writhes under the force of my body, as if she's deciding whether or not she wants to comply. I pull away, giving her enough space to turn around and do as she's been told.

Still, she hesitates.

"Turn around and put your hands on the truck." I say it slower this time. Even at her brattiest, a repeated command usually convinces her.

"Say please."

Oh, she's in rare form today. I don't beg, but I don't mind offering a little incentive.

"If you turn around and put your hands on the truck like a good girl, after I'm done spanking you, I'll spread you across my hood and worship your sweet little pussy with my mouth before I fuck you into tomorrow."

This is most definitely a concession on my part, not because I'm not dying to taste her, but because what I most want is to take her from behind so I can see my handprints on her ass while her perfect cunt juices around my throbbing cock.

"This is the second-best deal I've made today." She winks before she turns her hypnotic eyes away from me.

I immediately push her skirt up around her waist and pull her light-blue lacy thong to her knees.

She goes up onto her toes when I land the first slap on her toned ass. The whimper behind the breath she sucks in has my dick straining against my zipper. My second strike is a little harder than the first, but then I rub over her cheeks to soothe the sting.

The sight of her brazen nakedness outside tempts my hand to slide lower, to part her seam and slip through her arousal, plunge inside her pussy and ream her with as many fingers as I decide she needs, but delayed gratification is in both our best interests.

I spank her a few more times before my handprint becomes visible, pausing to soothe the heat rising on her skin between each one. Her agitation is obvious. She needs fewer breaks so she can adjust to the escalating stinging sensation until her body softens into it.

I'm noting her reactions, taking her needs into consideration, but unless she utters one of her safe words, I'm still calling the shots here.

I'll meet all her needs . . . when I think she's ready. I haven't misjudged her in the past.

As soon as I start to give her what she wants, welts begin to form at the edges of my handprints. Her pinkened skin becomes red. And her undulations aren't an attempt to escape, just a plea for a reprieve she doesn't actually want.

She's so close to sinking into the discomfort, embracing it, and evicting all the stress from her body.

Until she tells me to stop or calls red light (which are her safe words: stop, red light—explicit and unmistakable, just like her), I'm going to keep pushing her toward that release.

My palm is hot by the time her body relents. Her shoulders slide down, and her head gets heavy on her neck as the tension in her spine goes slack.

Her body's usual high-alert status has been disarmed entirely. She's pliable, as relaxed and vulnerable as she gets. And all I want right now is to make her feel good in a whole other way.

That's a lie. I want to see her completely naked, sprawled out on the hood of my truck like a centerfold, and then I want to make her feel good.

I waste no time stripping every piece of clothing from her satiated body. The sun warms the air as noon approaches, but there's still a slight chill in the wind. It's mostly died down, but a rogue cool breeze blankets her bare skin as I lay her back onto the warm metal.

I've spread the flannel shirt I keep in the truck beneath her, but warmth still radiates through the material.

The contrast in temperature sends shallow goosebumps down her arms and causes her nipples to harden. I brush over them with my thumbs, rolling them until they swell a little more before I splay my hands and drag them down her body to butterfly her legs.

I'd never call her modest, but I know this is pushing a boundary, even for her. She'd end me if I pulled my phone out to take a picture, so I take a snapshot with my eyes instead and commit it to memory—not like I could ever forget this image.

Her pussy is hot, slick, and subtly sweet beyond the initial familiar taste. If I were blindfolded and tasting it on toast, I'd know it was her.

A mockingbird squawks in the near distance as if it's scolding us.

Look away, buddy. I'm not stopping for you or any other creature.

And with that dare on the breeze, my aging boxer, Bo (short for Bocephus), crashes into my legs, nearly taking me down. I manage to hold my ground and shake him off. The dog makes his displeasure known as he ambles off. His grumbling growls make him sound like a disgruntled old man.

She laughs, and I yank her hips closer to the edge of the hood so I can get back to work.

I always love the sounds she makes when she comes, the way her whole body betrays her controlled composure. Rapture on full display.

And she doesn't hold back here—meddling birds and dogs be damned.

When she's fully depleted and lying in a state of bliss, I decide it's time to admire my handprints again.

She doesn't hesitate this time when I tell her to plant her hands on the truck, probably because her legs might be too unsteady to hold her upright if she doesn't brace herself.

As if I'd ever let her fall.

5
Glynnis

WAKING UP IN RHETT's bed feels way too comfortable. We met the night Mav proposed to Sabrina, nearly two years ago. I'd flown in specifically for the big event, under the guise of being here for the Derringer Wells show at Grin's.

This little town is an unlikely (in my opinion, at least) haven for famous music artists, but they flock here to record in Rhett's studio. And Grin's Pub has their favorite stage to unwind on after a session.

Mav's dad was something of a second dad to Rhett. Or maybe more like a cool uncle. At any rate, they went back a long way. Rhett would send artists over to play at Grin's after their recording sessions, and Mav's dad would promote the studio to any musicians passing through.

I used to think Grinberry Falls wasn't on the way to anywhere significant, but it turns out it's only a few hours from Austin. And a whole lot of musicians road-trip their way into Austin.

As a result of that early marketing partnership, Rhett's recording studio and Grin's Pub became destinations on the route, and for some of them, pitstops on the way to the top of the charts.

Rhett downplays it, but his studio is pretty legendary among recording artists.

All it took was for a few albums recorded there to go platinum—one reviving the career of a once famous country musician who was falling into obscurity—and voila!

Who knew musicians were so superstitious? Word spread that recording at Rhett's was the kiss of luck. His bookings went from primarily Texas artists to musicians coming from all over.

Despite the fact that I was initially wary of Mav, he definitely won me over when he looped me in on his proposal plans, and he hasn't given me any reason to dislike him since. He's honestly a hard guy not to like.

Some days, I think he's still deciding about me, but he's good for Sabrina, so he can be unsure about me for as long as it takes.

As far as waking up in Rhett's bed, well, that was never supposed to happen. Not once. But here I am, waking up next to him again with late afternoon sun streaming into his bedroom. I lost count long ago of how many times this has happened.

We see each other when I'm in town, but we've never put a label on it, and neither of us has asked for exclusivity. The thing is, once I experienced Rhett, other men failed to appeal.

He doesn't ask if I'm seeing anyone else, so I don't ask him either. It's an unspoken arrangement that keeps things light. No obligations, just a good time. We enjoy each other's company. Why ruin a good thing?

Rhett's twelve years older than me, which is perfect because I prefer older men. He has a few of my other preferable traits as well. Aside from being a stubborn ass on occasion, he's about as perfect as a man could get for me.

Not that I'm suggesting he's the man for me, just that what we've got going on is currently working in wondrous ways.

His eyes flutter open and catch me watching him sleep.

"You hungry?" he asks.

I check the time on my phone: three-thirty.

"It's too close to dinner for me to eat a full meal. I promised Sabrina I would have dinner with her and Mav tonight. I bet I could score you an invite."

"Like I won't invite myself." He rolls out of bed. "In the meantime, let's go grab a snack to hold us over."

If he's at dinner with us, there won't be any way for him to avoid hearing more about my contract on the little blue house. I have to tell Sabrina the latest development in bringing Sugar Lips to Main Street.

She's the one who convinced me to consider a location in Grinberry Falls in the first place.

As adamantly as Rhett and I will both stand our ground, we're also very good at avoiding a controversial subject for the sake of keeping the peace. I realize that's not the healthiest dynamic, but it keeps making it okay for me to wake up in his bed. And I'm not ready to stop doing that yet.

"What did you have in mind when you suggested a snack?" I ask as I redress myself, attempting to stretch the wrinkles out of my skirt. I'd complain about him wadding up my clothes, but given that we were in his yard when he took them off, there wasn't exactly a hanger available or a chair to lay them neatly over.

"Barbecue."

"That's not a snack."

"It is if you're as hungry as I am. Hurry up."

"I can't eat much. Sabrina's feelings will be hurt if she finds out I ate this late in the afternoon instead of waiting to eat with them. She's making lasagna."

"What time's dinner?"

"Seven. Ish."

"You can eat brisket now and still eat lasagna at seven. Ish. That's hours from now."

He smiles. I smile. This is another thing that is becoming way too comfortable. But not so much that I want to run from it, which is entirely uncomfortable in itself if I think about it too long.

I don't have to ask where we're headed for this snack. Rhett's truck could probably make the drive to Hickory Hill Barbecue on autopilot. It only took me one bite of their brisket to understand why it's his favorite, and we go back every time I'm in town.

It's impossible to only consume a snack-sized portion of tender smoked meat and roasted new potatoes and not-too-sweet coleslaw and Hickory Hill's homemade bread. I manage to say no to their peach cobbler, but only because I am a superhero among best friends.

I'm completely full when we leave.

"I ate too much." I groan as I step up into his truck.

"Wanna work it off?"

"I want to sleep it off."

Rhett clutches his chest like I've wounded him. "Are we really already at the stage where you'd rather sleep than have sex?"

"In my defense, we've had more sex than sleep today."

"That's fair. We've still got some time before we have to be at Mav and Sabrina's for dinner. You want to ride out to the creek?"

"Sure."

The creek is another place we go every time I'm in town. Chilcott Creek is wide and winding, surrounded by cypress trees whose craggy knees rise up from the water like ancient ruins. Their spindly branches reach out over the surface.

It's peaceful. A few kayakers may paddle by, but sometimes, we're the only ones there. We stave off disputes by avoiding disputable topics, but when we go to the creek, we always end up talking about meaningful things and sharing deeper truths than makes sense for two people so committed to avoiding commitment.

I can't seem to resist opening up to him at the creek. He lets his guard down there, too.

Looks like we might have the place to ourselves today. We walk to our favorite spot along the bank and sit near a mass of tangled cypress roots so thick they resemble a collapsed structure.

But they are the structure. They're the twisted mess that holds up and sustains all this beauty.

It's dusk, "magic hour," and all this rich golden light filtered onto the still water through ragged branches looks more like a painting than a real place.

I feel oddly at home here. As someone who left home for college at seventeen and only went back when I had to—until I never had to again—it's unsettling to feel at home anywhere. I love Scottsdale, but it doesn't feel like this.

Nowhere has ever felt like this.

The first time it hit me, it made me anxious and a little afraid, though I couldn't pinpoint what exactly I was afraid of. I got over it once I realized my weird response was all on me. Past me, anyway. I know now that I can love this place without being obligated to come back to it.

You'd think after so many years of therapy, my fight or flight response wouldn't be so easily triggered, that reality would stay more sharply in focus. When I stay super busy, it does.

It's when I slow down that things still feel scary sometimes. But I've learned to relax here with Rhett. I feel safe here now.

I sometimes wish I felt a little less comfortable. I've told Rhett things that make me wonder what came over me. The fact that he spills secrets to me here, too, helps.

It's fun to think there could be some greater power at work, weakening our resolve . . . something malevolent that can't help but attempt to steal power and control. Okay, maybe that's only fun for me.

Facing down demons is something that no longer gets my heart rate up, but dark and twisted possibilities intrigue way more than they could ever set me on edge.

I know if I were here with anyone else, my shields wouldn't fall like they do when I'm with him.

It's not just Chilcott Creek. It's Rhett Wilding, too, in all his malevolent glory.

I stare at the silhouette of his face as he stares at the water, lost in thought, glowing like some kind of god on the banks of a creek.

Wicked bastard.

6

Rhett

As soon as Glynnis told me about dinner at Mav and Sabrina's, I texted to tell him they should expect me, too. I don't mind inviting myself, but I don't want to be a surprise guest.

We're barely two steps over the threshold when she announces, "I bought a house on Main Street today!"

Mav already knows because he had a front-row seat to our conversation on his barstools, but he has apparently not bothered to tell his wife because her mouth hangs open in disbelief.

"You're moving here?" Sabrina asks. "Really? Do not fuck with me, Glynnie."

"No, of course, I'm not moving here. But Sugar Lips is, and I decided to buy instead of lease. I wanted to tell you sooner, but I didn't want to jinx it."

I hold my tongue. She announced it like it's a done deal, but signing a contract is only the first step to buying a place. That deal's got a way to go. It can still be jinxed.

The lasagna's good. Sabrina can cook, but she's on the road a lot for her job as a location scout for the film industry. As much as I never expected Mav to come back here, I damn sure never expected Sabrina to stay.

Love changes people. Kind of like when a car's odometer rolls to six digits. It'll still run, but it's probably not jumping off the line anymore.

Mav keeps throwing questioning glances at me while we eat. It's not like I can explain what the hell she was thinking when she decided to buy the place. He and I likely have all the same questions.

But Sabrina is charging ahead right along with her, enabling this whole fantasy of having a Sugar Lips location on Main Street.

I'm still not entirely clear on the business model. I know it all started when Glynnis invented a lip scrub that went viral. Now, you can apparently make your own custom lipstick and lip gloss in Sugar Lips. She sells her original lip scrub and new variations of it along with some lipstick and lip gloss. I may not know all the details about her lip spas, but I know they're damn popular. And profitable.

Apparently, women host parties there. Like book clubs, but for lip products, I guess. Oh, and they have people on staff who do that shit with the needles, too.

The things women do to themselves. I shake my head at the thought of it all.

"What's wrong with the lasagna?" Sabrina asks.

"Nothing. It's great."

"Then why are you shaking your head?"

"Just thinking. Not about the food."

She and her best friend exchange a knowing look, immediately followed by synchronized eye rolling.

Glynnis is smart, but did she do any market research at all? Who in Grinberry Falls is going to keep a Sugar Lips location afloat? I just don't think there are that many women around here with the inclination, not to mention the money, to frequent a place like that.

Then again, those new subdivisions at the edge of town are full of big houses with three-car garages and resort-style swimming pools in the backyards. And shopping centers are springing up like rain flowers.

Progress. That's one word for it. We can't stop what goes on outside the city limits, but we can at least preserve Main Street.

Anyway, out there among all that newness is where Sugar Lips belongs. Keeping it off Main Street would be doing her a favor.

There's not even enough parking for lip spa parties. Her customers would complain, leave bad reviews. That location would tank her business. A cute building won't offset the problems it would face.

She'll see reason. Eventually.

I just have to bring the obstacles to light strategically, at the right time and in the right way.

The women want to play one of those "how well do you know each other?" games after dinner. I'd rather snuggle a porcupine, but Mav says, "Sure, let's play."

Traitor.

7

Glynnis

I'VE REGRETTED MY ENTHUSIASM for this game more than once already. It's not that Rhett and I don't know a lot of these answers about each other, but sharing with other people how well we know each other is weird.

I remind myself it's just Mav and Sabrina, who definitely aren't going to be shocked by it. Still, I prefer not to put it on blast.

It's my turn, so I draw a card and read the question. "Who is the most likely to save a wounded animal?"

In unison, we all say, "Mav."

But I know Rhett is just as likely. I've seen him pull his truck over and free a fawn from a fence. Her leg was hung. He made sure she wasn't seriously injured and set her free. The satisfied smile on his face when the nervous doe watching from nearby joined her baby and led her away from the road gave him away.

When he got back in the truck, he shrugged and said, "Had to make sure she didn't need to be put down. It would've been cruel to leave her there for predators."

But when I went on and on about how adorable she was and how happy her mom was to see her set free, his smile widened. He's a softie under that aloof exterior.

His words were true. It would've been cruel to leave an injured animal vulnerable to predators, but he loved saving her. And I loved that he did it, too.

More than that, I loved knowing that he would've done it even if I hadn't been in the truck to see it. He acted without hesitation, on instinct.

Mav draws a card that obviously makes him tense. It was bound to happen with a game like this.

He hedges, tries to get out of reading it, but like the idiots we are, we insist he can't burn the card and draw another one. In our defense, we're all a little tipsy, not to mention high on constant laughter and the comfort of being with good friends—reckless in our confidence that we'll be immune to whatever poison the card sprays.

We taunt him, call him a chicken, tell him to man up already.

Mav gives in to our needling, takes a deep breath, and gives us exactly what we asked for.

"Who has the most emotional baggage?"

Yikes. Why didn't they just make a card that asks who's the most maladjusted jerk or the most likely to ruin someone else's life?

No one offers a response, but the sound of our sharp inhales as we flinch away from the question says all that needs to be said. It's an asshole question that only an asshole would answer. I could see someone being self-deprecating and falling on the sword to take one for the team.

Not anyone in this room, but there's probably a friend group out there somewhere where that could happen.

Rhett yawns, exaggerating it for effect. "I think it might be time to call it a night."

Silent agreement flows between us as we start packing up the game and carrying glasses to the kitchen.

I'm staying in the cottage, which Mav and Rhett refer to as the cabin. It's clearly a cottage with its beadboard siding and shuttered windows. No matter what we call it, it's my tiny home away from home.

Sabrina used to insist I stay in one of the guestrooms in the house, but after I stayed overnight at Rhett's one too many times, she finally just handed over a key to the cottage and told me to have him stay with me here instead.

She had an ulterior motive. If I'm already here, she doesn't have to wait for me to wake up and drive over from the ranch to spend the day with her.

As my best friend, she knows me well enough to know that Rhett's powers of persuasion might keep me at his ranch longer than I intend. At least if we're here, she can do battle with him on her home turf.

She's not afraid to barge into the cottage and tell him his time's up. It feels good to have someone fight for my time, but she doesn't need to. I'd never choose a man over our friendship.

Her timing's been off on a few occasions, though, forcing me to negotiate to keep him here a little longer, but she's not threatened by that. She just needs to make sure we're aware the clock is ticking.

We perform surprisingly well under pressure.

After we all say our goodbyes, Rhett walks me to the cottage. I try not to make any assumptions about him staying with me. We've spent practically the whole day together, so he may be ready for some space. I want to respect that because there are times when I'm the one who needs to pump the brakes.

But tonight, I wouldn't mind falling asleep with him again. That last question bothered me more than I want to acknowledge. I'm trying to ignore it, but it keeps re-piercing me like the stinging nettle I've finally learned to recognize.

The door's unlocked, so I open it as soon as we walk up, but I pause before I step inside.

"You were right. I could eat lasagna after gorging on barbecue. It's a good thing I don't live here. I'd gain twenty pounds a week."

"My offer to help you work it off still stands."

His kiss is deep and hungry. This isn't a goodbye kiss.

"Come on in, Daddy."

"I thought you'd never ask."

"Like you were actually waiting for an invitation."

"That's not really my style."

"I like your style."

"I know." He kisses me again, walking us into the cottage and pushing the door shut with his foot. He may not stay the whole night, but he'll stay long enough.

My phone buzzes as soon as I set it on the nightstand. I read the message while Rhett sits on the other side of the bed to take off his boots.

"Sabrina's not insulting me, is she?" He stands to face me.

I love the way he looks standing there. His smirk is playful. Sexy.

"Some might take it that way, but I'm sure you'd take it as a compliment."

"Come over here and let me compliment you."

I drop my phone and crawl across the bed to him.

He untucks his shirt as I reach the other side. I rise up onto my knees before he starts to unsnap it.

"That's my job."

His hands fall to let me take over.

My fingers grasp, and my lids lower in anticipation of one of my favorite sounds. I yank my hands in opposite directions, and the snaps pop in rapid-fire succession.

Mmmmm, yes. Play that on a loop at my funeral, please.

She loved a good popping sound—confetti launchers, champagne corks, pearl snaps . . .

Actually, I hope all three of those sounds are heard at my funeral. No tears, just laughter and happy popping sounds.

"What's that smile for?"

"Just thinking about my funeral."

"I wasn't planning on being quite that rough."

Gallows humor as foreplay is so on brand for us.

I play with the toggle of his zipper a bit, lowering it halfway and pulling it back up before I slowly pull it all the way down, smiling up at him the whole time.

8

Rhett

I'VE NEVER BEEN SO grateful for a session to wrap in my life. Some of the artists who record in my studio bring in their own engineer and producer, but I still work in the booth on a regular basis.

Sometimes, it's a great way to spend an afternoon. There are times I almost feel bad for taking their money. And then there are days like today, when I think I should've charged double because no amount of editing is going to make them sound as talented as they believe they are.

Who encourages these hacks? I blame reality TV. For a lot of wrongs if I'm being honest, but it's fucked up the music industry in unforgivable ways in my opinion.

Once again, people call it progress while I call bullshit. I can shout from my vantage point all day long, but it won't change a damn thing, so I shake their hands, take their money, and wish them well. The well wishes are sincere; I just don't think they're likely to come true.

But shit happens every day that I never would've predicted.

At least the sun's still shining when we walk outside. No time to enjoy it, though. I'm due at city hall in half an hour for a committee meeting. I'm not usually the one airing grievances, but I've got a load to get off my chest today.

Huck James is on my list. But he's not at the top.

That honor goes to the attorney in charge of creating the development commission and drawing up the Covenants, Conditions, and Restrictions—Eldon Roundtree.

It wasn't that long ago that I didn't even know what CC&Rs stood for. I used to happily mind my own business, but then I had to go and get a damn civic conscience and tap into some latent hometown pride I never knew was lurking within me.

If not for that "junk for a buck" store that tried to invade Main Street, I'd be sitting on my couch, about to crack open a beer and watch the Cowboys get their asses handed to them this afternoon instead of driving toward a fight.

I'd have been pissed off at the end of either event, but at least I don't personally know any of the Dallas players. Today, I've gotta go yell at men I've known my whole life.

I suppose the argument could be made that I don't have to yell at them, but I guarantee there's no argument that will stop me from doing it. This isn't just about unwanted changes on Main Street.

Their incompetence and disregard are going to mess with my personal life. Granted, there's no way to keep from making Twister mad from time to time, but I can usually make it up to her easily enough. But this? This paints me into a corner.

I can't stay out of her business and stay true to the organization that I spearheaded. There would be no Keep Grinberry Falls Local committee if I'd kept my head down and not looked beyond my own property lines.

What I wouldn't give for a fucking time machine.

Mav's truck is already parked in front of city hall. He's scrolling on his phone, completely oblivious to me walking up. I tap on his window, and he nearly jumps out of his skin.

He rolls down the window. "You scared the shit out of me."

"Guilty conscience?"

"For looking at football scores?"

"Sure, that's what you were looking at. Can I get in?"

"Yeah, we're early. Plenty of time for you to confess your latest sins."

"Fuck you." I walk around and get into the truck.

"What's on your mind?"

"You know what's on my mind. This meeting's gonna be a bloodbath."

"Any chance that might be a little dramatic?"

"Nope," I say. "Not from where I'm sitting."

Mav laughs. I'm glad I can amuse him with my troubles.

"She's sharp. You knew that. If anyone was going to find a loophole, it was going to be Glynnis. Frankly, nobody should be surprised."

"Some of us were surprised to learn she was even thinking about opening a location here." I stare at him accusingly.

"I was just as surprised as you. But it looks like she's bringing Sugar Lips to Main Street, one way or another."

"Oh, no she's not."

"Either I've misjudged the importance of your relationship with her, or you're a bigger dumbass than I ever would've imagined."

"She is important to me, okay? But I made a commitment, took a stand. I can't just shrink away from it to keep from rocking the boat with the woman in my life."

"I'd say that depends on how badly you want to keep that woman in your life."

"We're not married. We're not even engaged. We're not really anything you could put a label on."

"Give me a pen and paper. I bet I could come up with a whole list of labels that might fit."

"I've got a label for you right now."

"Eh, I bet that would probably fit, too. Doesn't change the fact that you're in a relationship, whether you're ready to acknowledge it or not."

"Fuck you."

"You've already used that one today. Try to be original for once in your life."

I pull on the door handle. "Let's go in and get this over with."

Word travels fast in this town. My ambush has already been foiled. Eldon meets us at the door to the conference room.

"Rhett, I've already gone over the restrictions in question, and I've got someone else reviewing them now. I know her attorney thinks they've found a loophole, but it's not as black and white as you've been led to believe."

"I'd feel better if it were, Eldon. Gray areas were never the goal when we started this venture."

Mav claps his hand on my back. "I think we should give legal counsel the time they need. Knee-jerk responses aren't what they get paid for."

"Wasn't aware they were getting paid for incompetence, either," I mutter as I walk away.

We go through all the parliamentary bullshit. I don't know why we need to hear the minutes from the last meeting. This isn't an open forum where citizens are coming to the podium. It's just a committee.

Or it would've been if our CC&Rs weren't so shockingly gray. How? Just how in the absolute godforsaken hell . . .

I reach for my water glass, not because I'm thirsty, but because it's impossible to grind my teeth if my mouth is full of water.

No time like the present. I open my mouth and unload my concerns.

Eldon shares the status of the legal review.

Huck shrugs.

Don't strain yourself to explain yourself.

No further business. That's how we're calling it?

Fine. Meeting adjourned.

Huck attempts to shake my hand on my way out. I don't often deny a man a handshake, but he doesn't want me to touch him right now. Surely, he knows this.

"Didn't realize you had the property on the market," I say.

"I don't know what to tell you, Rhett. She made a good offer, and I'm not using the space. There wasn't exactly a long list of people inquiring about it. An empty building sitting on Main Street wasn't doing the town any favors.

"You were supposed to bring it to the committee before you finalized anything."

"That's what I thought, too, but she pointed out some things that made sense. She'd already had her attorney review it. She wanted a decision. Hell, I didn't go to law school."

"You don't say."

He drops his hand. "We'll still have more than ninety-percent local occupancy. Why are you making this such an issue? Is it personal? Because it feels like it might be personal, Rhett."

"You signed on to adopt those CC&Rs, Huck. You can't just ignore them and do whatever you want."

"But that's what I'm trying to tell you. I wasn't ignoring a rule. The rule simply doesn't exist."

"That's up to the attorneys to decide. We've already established you didn't go to law school."

"As far as I know, neither did you."

"I'm not the one who sold a property on Main Street."

I storm out and drive straight to the creek. And park right next to her car.

Apparently, this day's not done surprising me yet.

9
Glynnis

I LOOK OVER MY shoulder when I hear tires pulling to the side of the road.

How'd he know I was out here? He slams his truck door more aggressively than I expect. His grimace as soon as he does it tells me he didn't expect to do it either.

"You stalking me?" I yell.

"You could be stalked by worse."

"Maybe. How nefarious are your intentions?"

"I'd advise you to run, but I don't have the energy to chase you right now."

"Rough day?"

He sits next to me. "Not the best I've ever had, but far from the worst. How about you?"

I shrug. "It wasn't bad. Spent most of it shopping with Sabrina."

"Shopping and spending time with Sabrina are two of your favorite pastimes. What made you decide to come to the creek alone?"

"Needed to think. Sorry if I'm encroaching on your private thinking spot, but you're the one who introduced me to it."

"I don't own the creek."

"Just Main Street?"

Dammit, I promised myself I wasn't going to do that.

Fortunately, he refuses to take the bait.

"I never asked how long you were going to be in town. Sorry about that. It wasn't that I didn't care when you were leaving."

"You don't have to keep up with my schedule. I'm glad you want to see me when I get here, but I never expect any big send-off."

"You didn't answer my question."

"I'm driving back tomorrow morning."

"Quick trip."

"I had a specific purpose this time. It was a business trip."

"Right." He pulls up a few blades of grass and examines them like he's intently looking for something before he drops them and wipes his hand on his jeans.

"It was nice to mix in a little pleasure, though," I say, hoping to make it clear I'm not going to harp on the Main Street thing. I've already won that battle, anyway, so there's no point in being petty.

"Always happy to be a part of your pleasure."

Is he saying it wasn't pleasurable for him? Because that's a damn lie.

He smiles and brushes a section of hair off my cheek. "You definitely make my life more pleasurable when you're in town."

I swear, sometimes he can read me like a book. He defused that impending blow-up with ease. It's hard to be mad at him. Hard to stay mad, anyway.

But I'm not out here because I'm mad. Sad? Maybe. It's been a long time since I've had to deal with that. Sad is my least favorite negative emotion. Give me anger any day. I can work with anger.

Sad's a ruthless bitch, who shows up when nothing has even gone wrong. At least when I'm pissed off, I usually know why.

"Any chance you can stay a few more days?"

"I've got a therapy appointment day after tomorrow. I could do it as a televisit, but I prefer talking to her in person."

"That makes sense. I'd probably prefer that, too. If I ever felt the itch to go to therapy."

"It's not for everyone."

"You don't have to be nice about it, Twister. I'm aware I could probably use it."

"I'm not saying you need it, but I don't think it hurts anyone to try it. What's the worst that could happen? You go once and make an informed decision?"

He pulls more grass.

I wish he hadn't asked me to stay. I was perfectly fine leaving until he did that.

"You got plans with Sabrina tonight?" he asks.

"No."

"Will you spend your last night in town with me?"

"Yeah."

"At my place?"

"Oh."

Why did that question unnerve me for a beat? I've stayed at the ranch before.

"If it'll cause a problem between you and Sabrina, I get it. I don't want to make waves there."

"She'll still be asleep when I leave in the morning, anyway. And she won't be shocked to hear I'm spending the rest of my time here with you."

"The two of you've been friends for a long time."

"Since college. I showed up in Chicago, fresh from the outskirts of Florida sugarcane fields with stars in my eyes. Chicago had been my dream escape city since I was a kid, and I just knew I was going to fit right in. She had to teach me how to use the trains. She introduced me to food I'd never heard of. Taught me how to handle the snow and literally gave me a coat because I didn't own one. I probably would've just skipped class every time it snowed if not for her. She's responsible for my degree and my love of giardiniera."

"Big honors."

"She acts tough, but she's a caretaker."

"You had the acting tough part in common."

"Except I actually am tough."

"I know. Hard to believe how long you and I've known each other."

"It's creeping up on a while," I say.

"We probably know a lot more about each other than most people think."

"Yeah," I agree. "I'm sure they think we just spend all our time with our clothes off."

"I guess Sabrina knows better."

"She knows more than most."

"Does she know you're out here?"

"Don't worry. Your secret place is safe with me."

He laughs. "Chilcott Creek's not exactly a secret."

"You plan on pulling up all the grass in one day?"

"No. I guess I'll leave myself something to do on my next visit." He stands.

I'm not sure I'm ready to leave, but I stand, too.

He instantly wraps his arms around me as if he knows I could use a hug. I hate that, but it feels nice to be held, so I hug him back and hang on a little longer than I usually do.

"Come on. I'll cook you dinner," he says.

"You mean you'll fire up the grill. Are we having burgers?"

"We can have whatever you want. As long as it's in my freezer and can be cooked on the grill."

I follow him back to his place, and Bo runs to me the moment we walk in the door. He's never run to me instead of Rhett.

"Oh, I see how it is," Rhett says. "I know she's prettier than me and she smells better, but I'm still the one who buys your food and pays your vet bills, buddy."

Bo looks over at his owner, but he presses his body against my legs, almost as if he's protecting me from Rhett.

"I think you're being shut out," I say.

"Cock-blocked by my own dog."

"If he were a female dog, you'd have to say clam-jammed."

"Jesus Christ. I never needed to know that phrase."

"Stick with me. I'll teach you all kinds of things."

"Oh, yeah? You're the teacher now?"

"You see me as the student?" I ask.

"That's not exactly the word I'd use."

"Oh, okay. I thought maybe you were initiating a little role playing."

"If I were, you would definitely be the student."

"I'd probably behave terribly in your class."

"To hell with the grill. We'll order a pizza later."

He takes my hands and pulls me forward, forcing me to step over Bo, who cedes his position but grumbles all the way to his bed.

His owner growls a little on the way to his, too.

What starts out playful ends up being incredibly intimate. This is fairly new for us. And entirely new for me. I never would've accepted this kind of closeness with anyone else, and I damn sure wasn't expecting it to show up with Rhett.

The ravenous, hot, and heavy stuff is our signature style, but lately, no matter how we start, things keep slowing to a more leisurely pace where the kisses last longer and the eye contact reaches a deeper place. We don't always stay in those moments until the end, but they always show up.

He's definitely the only man who's ever made me drench his sheets while being this tender. It's hard to put up a strong front when your body gives you away like that. It doesn't hurt his ego any, I know that.

"God, I love when you do that."

"I love when you make me do that. But given how often it's happening you might need to invest in a waterproof blanket."

"I wouldn't even know where to get one of those. Towels work."

I hate sleeping on his scratchy towels. "I'll buy you the blanket."

"Get one for your place, too."

He's only visited me in Scottsdale twice in the two years we've known each other, but he made that suggestion as if we split our time equally between our places.

"You can just bring yours if you come back to my place."

"I'll come back to your place, but I'm not packing a blanket. Buy two."

"Is that an order?" I tease.

"No, but this is. Roll over."

My body twists with no conscious effort. His hands stay on me, acting as a guide to position me exactly the way he wants me.

I love the way he never forces me to make decisions. He takes control, but I know I can ask for whatever I want and refuse what I don't. There's just rarely anything that I want to refuse him.

He runs a hand up my back, pausing at the top to urge my shoulders toward the bed. I press my cheek to the mattress and stretch my arms long above my head, moaning when he runs his hands back down my spine.

This is one of my favorite positions, but not one where he expresses tenderness. I brace myself for the first powerful thrust, and then I begin to match his forward momentum with backward thrusts of my own.

It's our farewell fuck, and we both strive to make those memorable.

There's never a future date set in stone. This could be the last time we see each other for months. I'll miss him for a few days, but then I'll adjust and return to my regularly scheduled life.

10

Rhett

S HE'S BEEN GONE FOR nearly two weeks. I've been staying busy with time in the booth, doing some needed repairs on the house, and fishing. This weekend, I'm headed to a bluegrass festival. She joined me last year, but she said she's got too much on her plate to get away right now.

I tried the argument that that's when you most need to get away, but I didn't push too hard.

It'll be fine. I know most of the artists who are performing. It's not like I'll be all alone. I may even play in a band or two for a few sets. I don't play much anymore, but I'm not too rusty to get on stage. Somebody always needs a last-minute musician.

It was never my dream career. I like being musician adjacent, but it's fun to switch sides every now and then.

There's a good chance somebody will need an engineer at some point, too. I've worked with some of these acts before, so I'm familiar enough to jump in.

I won't have any problem staying busy at the festival. And when I'm not, I'll just enjoy the music and catch up with people. It'll be a good weekend.

It'd be better if she could've come.

We don't talk every day, but at least a few times a week. She hasn't mentioned the loophole that she trusted when she signed that contract.

It looks like her attorney interpreted it correctly, so I haven't brought it up either. Just because she can move forward with bringing Sugar Lips to Main Street doesn't mean there won't be trouble ahead.

Inspections could still tank the deal.

Part of me likes knowing she'd be around more often if everything passes inspection and the appraisal checks out. She's pretty hands-on with her business. I don't believe for a minute that she wouldn't oversee the renovation closely.

Sabrina has already said that Glynnis likes to pick out every last detail, right down to what brand of toilet paper goes in the bathrooms.

She has managers who run all three of her existing locations, but she apparently handles all the upfront decisions on her own and then hands over the reins to let them maintain what she's established.

Her flagship store in Scottsdale is her baby. She still works behind the counter in that one fairly often, but she stays pretty busy with admin stuff behind the scenes.

I understand why it's still fun for her to meet her customers and do the job that she created sometimes, though.

People like to know the face behind the business, but it's also good to stay in touch with your roots. Remembering what brought you to where you are makes it a whole lot easier to hold on to what you've got.

Building something worthwhile takes work, but holding on to it takes more.

11

Glynnis

I'VE MADE A LIST of all the things I need to get done while I can still be in Scottsdale full-time over the next several weeks. Once my little blue house gets all the green lights, I'll need to be in Grinberry Falls for a while.

Mav and Sabrina's cottage is going to be more than a place to sleep. It'll truly be my home away from home during the build-out.

I'm dying to bring a general contractor onboard and get going with it all. I've got big plans for that little house.

My therapist's eyes went wide while I told her all of my ideas. She's always cautioning me about taking on too much, but this is the most exciting part of a new launch. I thrive on the chaos and deadlines.

She knows this about me; she must've forgotten since I opened my last location. It'll be frustrating and fun and hard and rewarding—all the things at once. I prefer to have life coming at me like a spontaneously-combusting keg of Roman candles. Keeps me on my toes.

But today, I've got a desperately-needed massage on my calendar.

I saw the same massage therapist for years, but she left Arizona for Ireland a few months ago. It was a permanent move, not a vacation. I held out hope that she'd change her mind and come back for as long as I could, but my shoulders can't wait any longer for the pummeling they need.

Please let this guy have hands as strong as Anya's—and not be afraid to use his strength. Sometimes, men hold back, afraid they'll hurt me. I'm already hurt. That's why I show up on their table. Healing pain is what I'm there for.

I've never asked Rhett to give me a massage, but I know his hands are strong enough. When he rubs my back, it's never forceful, though. He might increase the pressure if I asked. I can't think of a request he's ever denied me.

I shake my head to banish the thought of Rhett's hands on my body. That's definitely not what I need to be thinking about during a massage. This new massage therapist deserves a fair shot.

I'M NOT TOO DISAPPOINTED to book a second appointment, but it wasn't my best massage ever. I also failed miserably at not thinking about Rhett—nonsexual thoughts—but comparing any other man's hands to his is never going to go well for the other guy.

It's a good afternoon to work in Sugar Lips. I've got a party of six, all first-timers coming in. Virgins are my favorite.

I run home to shower and get ready for work. It's not like I don't work at some point every day, whether I go into the spa or not, but being there still feels like going to work in a totally separate way.

A familiar song plays on my streaming service in the car, and I turn it up. This album was recorded at Wilding Studios. Rhett was the engineer. I never once thought about how an album or a song was produced before I met him.

I'm positive he never even knew a lip spa could be a thing before he met me. He's still a little fuzzy on how it can possibly be a real business, but he's supportive. I haven't talked to him in a few days.

He's probably on his way to the bluegrass festival. That was a fun road trip with him last year. The festival was a blast, and he's easy to travel with.

One of my injectionists, Macey, is leaving for the day as I walk in. She's a nurse, so she only works here part-time. Her other job is in a plastic surgery clinic. This is my only location that employs three injectionists, and one of the other two also has another job. It's not uncommon.

"Hey, Glynnis! I saw you were on the schedule today." She stops for a hug. "How was Texas?"

"I was going to wait to make the announcement after I close on it, but I'm dying to tell everyone. Sugar Lips is headed to Grinberry Falls, Texas! Location number four will open later this year."

"I had no idea you were going to scout a location for a new spa! That's amazing. Congratulations."

"Macey, I can't wait for you to see it. It's right on Main Street in the cutest little blue house. It screams small-town, but of course, the inside will be all Sugar Lips."

"That little town better get ready to be wowed."

"This one is going back to basics. No procedures, at least not in the beginning. I'm keeping the budget tight until we've tested the market, but I'm buying the building. The town is growing fast, so I feel good about it."

"This is so exciting. If the market doesn't support it, you can always lease the building out to a boutique or a salon."

"Exactly. I knew you'd get it. You headed to the clinic?"

"Hospital. We've got a jaw reconstruction this afternoon."

"Sounds intense. Good luck."

"It'll be great," she says. "Reconstructions are my favorite."

"I'm glad there are people like you willing to do it, but I can't imagine. Drive safe."

"Always."

One of the employees behind the counter is new. This is his first week, and today is the first time I've worked with him. I've heard nothing but good things, so I'm looking forward to it.

"Hi, Emma. How's it going, Noah?"

"Hi, Glynnis." The manager, Emma bounces on her toes, which can only mean she has something exciting to share. "Noah booked his first party yesterday, and he sold three signature kits. And then he sold two more this morning!"

Noah smiles sheepishly and nods.

Our signature kit includes two lip scrubs, a lipstick and a gloss from our signature color collection, and a hydrating lip mask. It retails for one-thirty, and it's not on sale right now. Aside from the create-your-own-color custom duo, the signature kit is our highest-ticket item.

"Way to go, Noah."

I knew he'd be a natural for sales. I can always tell.

"Thanks, Glynnis. Did you just tell Macey you're opening a location in Texas?"

"I did. I'll keep everyone updated, but our fourth location should open there this year."

They congratulate me, and then I head back to the office so they can help the customer who's just walked in.

I let my fingertips trail over the swirly design of the hall wallpaper. I really, really love this place. The sads are completely gone now. Maybe I just needed to get back here and remind myself of what's possible. It was probably just the natural fear of expanding. When I opened this location, I was afraid, too.

Pushing through fear is the only way forward. Sugar Lips is marching forward, and I don't intend to let anyone stop it.

Emily buzzes me when the party arrives, and I come out to welcome them.

It's a rowdy group, which I love. Parties don't include injections of any type, so Noah hands each of them our wine and champagne menu while Emily handles nametags. I greet everyone and start committing names to memory.

Alcohol is another thing our Grinberry Falls location may not have at first. Something tells me Texas liquor laws might be a pain in the ass.

For all I know, Grinberry Falls may have its own restrictions around it, too.

It wasn't mentioned in the Keep Grinberry Falls Local regulations, but that committee's focus isn't on limiting business types or services; it's all about keeping outsiders like me from corrupting the place with any business at all.

I bet Mav would give me an idea of what to expect on the liquor laws. So far, he seems neutral about me opening a location there.

When I'm ready to add cosmetic procedures, there will be regulations to navigate for that, too. It'll be a process, but we'll get there.

We'll open as a storefront and grow into our full services.

I watch with pride as Emily and Noah get the women settled. They're good. It takes strong people skills to do this job.

Sugar Lips is a beauty-based business, but really, it's about so much more than lips. We cater to the whole person. It's a place to be in community with friends, to feel welcome, and be pampered for a little while.

The goal is for every customer to feel better about themselves when they leave than when they walked in, whether they buy anything or not. Not making a sale on their first visit doesn't mean they won't come back.

People remember how you make them feel. That's what brings them back, even after they become regulars. The best products and services in the world won't sustain a business if people don't feel good about buying them.

We all crave connection, even in places we don't realize it matters.

It always matters.

12

Rhett

I MISSED HER BEING at the festival with me, but Twister told me this morning that she's closing on her little blue house tomorrow. It feels like she just signed the contract yesterday, but it's been a month.

Every inspection is cleared. The appraisal flew through underwriting with no issues. I'm happy for her because she's so happy, and I loved hearing that she's staying in town for a few weeks after closing.

She's never been here for that long, and it's been too damn long since I've seen her.

I don't care that the only reason she's staying is to meet with a general contractor and get the buildout started. As long as I get to see her, that's all that matters.

She's flying in tomorrow morning since she has the closing set for two p.m. That means she should be done in time for dinner. I offered to pick her up at the airport, but she wants to rent a car since she'll be here so long this time. It's nearly two hours away, and I was looking forward to having that extra time with her, but she had her mind made up.

I'll take her out to dinner to celebrate and then keep her with me for as long as she'll let me.

My phone buzzes with a message from one of the ranch hands. He says they're moving pastures today and they're short a man. They'll be moving across the creek bed, so they could use my help if I'm not busy.

I grew up ranching, but I lease most of my land and let somebody else work it. That wasn't the life for me, but I still like wide open spaces. And I still know how hard the work is.

There's nobody in the studio, and I don't want to leave these guys in a bind.

Looks like I'm about to saddle up and push cows for the rest of the day.

Trudy's Diner is packed. Never dreamed there'd come a day when I'd have to wait for a table here. I lurk near the bar, hoping a stool will open up. Bar seating is still first-come, first-serve.

Trudy's daughter, Merilee looks up from sliding fresh pies into the case and smiles.

"You going to keep putting up with this place forever?" I ask, knowing she's only here to help her mom, but she worked hard to get through nursing school. It seems a little unfair for her to still be pulling shifts here. "I'd think nursing would keep you busy enough."

She shrugs half-heartedly. "Some days, waitressing is my sanity break. And trust me, I'm as surprised by that as you are."

"Nursing's a tough gig."

"It's not the job itself; it's all the constantly changing paperwork and politics of working in a hospital. It's a lot. I just want to put my patients first, take care of them, make sure I'm supporting my coworkers . . . the way it should be."

She looks way more tired than anyone in their twenties ever should.

"Do you think you'd like working in a private doctor's office better?"

"Maybe. I just always envisioned myself working in a hospital."

"Visions can change."

She smiles again. "I know."

Before she can say anything else, another waitress pulls her aside to whisper something in her ear. Merilee rolls her eyes and reassures her that she'll take care of it. It's clear Merilee thinks whatever frantic thing the other woman has just told her is ridiculous.

I bet every employee here comes to her for everything. She's always been Trudy's second in command. By the time she was a teenager, I have no doubt she could've run this place by herself. I hate hearing that she's not happy.

Mav and Sabrina come in, and I tell the hostess to add them to my name on the list and seat us together. There's no sense in waiting on separate tables, and I hate to eat alone.

After we place our orders, Sabrina looks me in the eye and says, "You know that Glynnie is going to be around a lot over the next several months, right?"

"Yeah, I know. I won't steal all of her time, I promise."

"I'm not worried about that. I'm worried about the two of you living in the same town for the first time."

"Are you saying this town's not big enough for the both of us?"

Mav laughs. "What town is?"

"What I'm saying is that this could be a turning point. You're both used to spending such short amounts of time together. This will be the first time you've had the option to see each other whenever you want, and I'm just wondering how you feel about that."

"She'll be busier than ever, still running her business while getting the new location ready. She's going to have a lot going on."

"Yeah, and when she has a lot going on, she can get hyper-focused on things. Sometimes, things that wouldn't otherwise matter so much."

"You don't have to prepare me for her, Sabrina. I'll be able to handle her when she's stressed."

"You'll probably learn a lot of new things about each other."

"You realize we know each other pretty well, right?"

"I realize you think you know her well, Rhett."

"I look forward to getting to know her better then. How's that?"

She sighs. "I don't know how to explain what I'm trying to say."

Mav closes his hand over hers. "I think he gets it, Brina."

"You're worried I'll hurt her. And you're worried if she and I have a big blowup that ends things between us, it'll make things weird for all of us."

"Yes, and yes," she says. "Don't break her heart. And don't break up the band, either, Yoko."

She grins, but I can see the worry trapped in her eyes. I can't give her any guarantee about what might happen with Twister and me. Hell, I can't give myself any guarantee.

Mav changes the subject, and we enjoy our dinner.

My legs are stiff when we stand to leave. It's been a while since I worked as hard as I did today. I'll be more physically active with Twister in town. That thought puts a smile on my face. She can't get here fast enough for the other reactions it inspires.

As tired as I am tonight, I'd happily stay awake until dawn with her. Goddamn, I wish she was already here.

13
Glynnis

MY HAND IS CRAMPING by the time I'm done signing all the closing documents, but when the agent congratulates me and puts the keys in my hands, the pain disappears. It's a done deal. The little blue house on Main Street is all mine.

I drive straight from the closing to meet with the general contractor I've hired. I talked to three GCs at length before I chose him, but it was all done by phone. I'm looking forward to meeting him in person.

There's not a parking space to be had in front of the house, but there's a small lot in the back. Thank goodness. Otherwise, my customers would have to park down the street. Not that there's any section of Main Street where parking is plentiful.

I turn onto my narrow driveway and go around to the gravel lot in the back. There's a truck already parked backed here. That's a good sign. I appreciate punctuality.

When the driver steps out, I'm taken aback for a moment. He's so young. Then I realize he's probably the guy's son or an employee. I thought I was meeting with Enzo Torres alone, but I don't mind if he brought someone else along.

I extend my hand and introduce myself. "Hi. I'm the owner, Glynnis Ramsey."

"I figured you must be," he says, shaking my hand. "I'll be confirming some measurements while we walk through and talk about your ideas, but I promise I'll be listening. I just think better when I have actual numbers to work with."

He leans back into his truck and grabs a rolling tape measure. I'd never seen one of those prior to my first renovation, but now I own one. They're handy. He also clips a retractable handheld tape measure to his belt.

"I know you said there will be a long counter upfront, and you want marble. Before we talk materials, I want to be clear on the dimensions for that. I may have a better option in mind."

Wait. He's Enzo? Holy shit. I opened my first Sugar Lips when I was twenty-five, so I try not to put expectations on anyone based on their age, but it takes a lot of knowledge, not to mention experience, to oversee a construction project. I know I'm not building from the ground-up, but still.

I take a steadying breath and remind myself how much he impressed me when we talked. He has the knowledge. I've seen his portfolio. He's done some amazing projects, and his references were stellar.

There's no way for me to know his age without asking, and it's not really any of my business. I just need to get over the initial shock.

And he needs to get over thinking he's going to change my mind about the marble countertop.

"The counters in my other locations are all the same dimensions, but those spaces are longer than this one. I may have to come up with a new configuration to work with a square building."

"That's why we measure. If you start to feel overwhelmed at any point in the project, just remember, you're not doing this alone. You talk. I listen. We make decisions. Deal?"

"Deal."

We walk toward the house.

"I should probably confess that I can be a bit of a perfectionist," I say.

He nods. "You already told me that. And I'm the same, so it'll be fine."

I put my key in the lock and turn the knob for the very first time. Going in the back door isn't as dramatic as entering through the front, but it's still incredibly satisfying.

"You should also know that my tone can get a little severe when I'm in the zone," I warn. "I have a tendency to snap at people when I'm thinking through a problem."

"Yep. We covered that, too. I won't take it personally, I promise."

"If there's a problem with a supplier or a delivery, I'll probably fly off the handle before I can center myself and accept that there's nothing we can do about it. I know those things happen, but I still get frustrated when the schedule has to change. I won't mean to take it out on you, but—"

"Breathe, Glynnis." He looks around the kitchen as if his eyes are already drawing up plans. "If I think you're out of line, I'll let you know. But I'm used to managing clients' expectations. And taking the brunt of their anger when things don't go exactly as planned. It's all part of the process. Nothing sticks to me. As long as you're happy when it's done, that's all that matters. If we butt heads along the way, we'll get through it."

Who the hell is this calm and measured at his age? I sure wasn't. I'm both impressed and a little resentful. But I'm more convinced by the minute that I chose the right GC.

"Just don't yell at my subcontractors. If you have a problem with somebody, you bring it to me. I'll handle it."

Oh, well, there's our first bump in the road. If I have a problem with somebody, I like to yell at them directly. I take another deep breath.

"I'll do my best."

He stares at me like he knows I don't mean it.

"Remember, if you run off a subcontractor, that portion of the job stops until I can find someone else. This whole area is booming right now. Subs are busy. So, if you feel inclined to piss one off, make sure it's worth the delay it might cause."

He definitely knows how to reason with me. This is a useful reminder because I don't like delays And I damn sure don't want to be the reason for one.

"No yelling at subcontractors. Got it."

"It's going to be in your best interest not to confront them in any tone." Enzo's tight smile tells me he's aware it might happen, anyway. This guy's got good people skills.

He's cute, too. I wonder if he's single. Not for me, of course. He's entirely too young for me, but I do love playing matchmaker.

I might have two projects to work on.

We walk the whole house, and he notes measurements of everything from the square footage of each room to the height and width of the windows. He knocks on the walls that I want to tear down, backs up and repeats his steps on the floor in a few areas, and flips all the light switches.

I don't ask questions whenever he makes a concerned face as he does these things. I'm not sure I want to hear any of his initial fears. It's probably best to let him gather his thoughts before he shares them with me, anyway.

I know from experience there's no point in getting upset about a problem before it's confirmed. Besides, the inspections and appraisal didn't find any problems.

He asks me a few questions, mostly about each room's purpose. I walk him through a more in-depth description of what Sugar Lips actually does. When I explain about the room I hope will ultimately serve as a procedure room, he squints and chews his bottom lip. Most men have a visceral reaction to the mention of lip injections.

I'm so eager to move on to discussions about materials and finishes, but I know we have to get the structures in place first. This is the hardest part for me. I want it done right, though, so I call on what little patience I have.

Before we leave, he explains his next steps, and in what order I'll see subcontractors. The demo will come first. It'll get worse before it gets better. I know that, but it probably doesn't hurt for me to hear him say it.

"I'll get my subs in here over the next few days and hopefully, apply for permits this week. Grinberry Falls has a lot of new houses going up, and those developers are all in line ahead of us, but the city makes a point not to let the big homebuilders keep small contractors at the back of the line for too long. They'll pull local applications and move them up periodically, so I don't expect it to take more than a month."

"A month? I'm only here for a few weeks."

"There won't be much happening. If you want to be around to see construction get underway, you might want to go home and come back once we start swinging hammers."

"I thought there'd be hammers swinging by next week."

"In Grinberry Falls? The only thing that moves fast around here are the trains that roll through town."

"It never took more than a week to get a permit on my other remodels."

"Glynnis, I hate to be the one to break it to you, but Grinberry Falls ain't Scottsdale."

"No, it really ain't."

"Didn't you tell me you've only remodeled spaces in new buildings for your other locations?"

"Yeah, they all opened in brand-new buildings. I guess that makes a difference."

"It definitely makes a difference. We've got to get approved for new plumbing and electrical, removing walls, moving the gas line outlet in the kitchen. The house is small, but you're making big changes. This one's going to be a whole different process."

"Okay. That makes sense. Thanks, Enzo. Keep me updated."

"Every step of the way." He starts for the back door, but stops and turns around after a few steps. "You really got permits in a week in Scottsdale?"

"Yep."

"Huh. Maybe I need to relocate. Even for a buildout within new construction, that's crazy fast. You think there's any chance your GC called in a favor?"

"It's possible." I know exactly what he means, and if I'm being honest, my GC there was sort of cagey about some things, and he could be a little scary. That didn't stop me from yelling at him, but he did look pretty stunned the first time I did it. He never seemed too comfortable with direct eye contact either.

"Does anybody in Grinberry Falls owe you any favors?" I ask.

"I'm not made for doing business like that."

"Damn."

"Tell me about it."

I walk through the house once more after Enzo's gone. He probably envisioned framing and wires as he went from room to room, but I see colorful rugs on refinished floors and wallpaper on new walls, gleaming glass cases, and a velvet loveseat.

When I look up in the living room that will become our sales and party space, I envision the perfect chandelier already hanging there. It can't be hung for weeks—or months, apparently—but now that I've seen it in my head, I have to hunt it down.

I hope Sabrina's in the mood to traipse through antique shops with me this week. And maybe next. I'm on a mission.

There is no time limit on this search. I'll know it when I see it, but I won't rest until that happens.

It would be easier to buy something new that was made to look old, but that's not the vibe I want in this location. I want real vintage pieces from chandeliers to loveseats.

Maybe I'll find an antique red phone with a curly cord. I've always wanted one of those. I can already see it on the shelf with our signature reds, sitting next to the postcard Rhett gave me. That gorgeous postcard needs an ornate gold frame. Adding that to my mental list now, too.

Let the scavenger hunt begin.

Before I leave, I take a moment to lean against the doorframe between the hallway and the living room, arranging furniture in my mind. The room will be bigger because we're downsizing the kitchen to be more of a kitchenette. That's all we really need, and I need the extra space for the party table.

Enzo had some good ideas about the counter configuration. I've sent him pics of the main public spaces in my other locations so he can see why I need so many shelves and cabinets along the wall. We may have to use the wall on the right side here instead of the left.

For practical purposes, it makes no difference which side of the store the products are on, but emotionally, it's difficult to change my standard layout. I'm so used to customers shopping on the right and partying on the left.

He offered to move the front door to keep this one formatted like the other locations, but that's an unnecessary expense. I make my share of emotional decisions, but I'm generally more realistic when finances are involved.

It'll all be fine once the hammers are swinging and I can see progress—however many months from now that starts.

I hate being in limbo. I'm restless, and it's only day one of the wait. I either need to drag Sabrina on a shopping expedition, or I need to see Rhett.

There's a sparkling, three-tiered chandelier and a shiny red phone with my name on it out there somewhere.

Sabrina now, Rhett later.

She'll commiserate and rage with me over the ridiculousness of waiting a month or more for permits. He'll just be all calm and cool about it.

He's good at getting me out of my head, and I need that sometimes. But not right now.

14

Rhett

I**T'S OFFICIAL. TWISTER OWNS** a shop on Main Street. Mav told me it was a done deal right after she let Sabrina know.

I got a message from her about an hour later. Apparently, she and Sabrina are out shopping for a chandelier. Seems a little early for that if you ask me, but asking me is about the last thing she'd do when it comes to her new location.

She did agree to go to dinner with me after she gets back to the cabin. I'm just waiting on the greenlight to head over there.

Derringer Wells is in the studio, but he brings his own team these days. His sessions sometimes last until late in the night. I don't worry about leaving him to lock the place up on his own.

Aside from knowing him since he was just a hopeful kid, he's my neighbor now. He's still just a kid in my eyes, but his ranch starts where mine ends. The kid's doing all right for himself.

I hold the passenger-side door open on my truck and call for Bo. He comes running because he knows we're about to do his favorite thing.

"Load up!"

He leaps up into the truck like there's nothing to it. We ride around back roads for about fifteen minutes, his head hanging out the window with his ears flapping in the wind. He'll chase birds and squirrels all day long, but nothing makes him happier than going for a quick ride. It also calms him down, so I try to drive him around a bit before I leave him in the house for too long.

He's fine outside for a while during the day as long as it's not too hot, but I don't leave him outside all night. Anytime there's a chance I might stay gone overnight, he gets a ride before he gets cooped up inside.

I have no idea if I'll end up staying at the cabin tonight, but I'd like to. What I'd really like is for her to stay at my place, but she only allows herself a limited number of overnight visits at the ranch. She's never said as much, but I can see the gears turning when I ask her to stay here, always weighing something before she answers.

If she says anything at all in the way of explaining her hesitation, she claims it's to keep from upsetting Sabrina. That may be part of it, but I know there's more to it.

She finally calls as I'm stepping out of the shower.

"Did you find your chandelier?" I ask.

"No. But I'm craving pizza. Is it okay if I pick one up and bring it to your place?

"I was planning to take you out to celebrate."

"I'd rather stay in."

"Okay, we'll go to dinner another night. No olives."

"Not on your half, maybe, but I'm definitely getting olives. Do you have wine?"

"I have wine, beer, whatever you want."

"I love when you're so accommodating."

"When have I ever not accommodated you?"

Shit. She's going to throw the Keep Grinberry Falls Local committee in my face. It's my fault for giving her the perfect opening . . .

"Nothing comes to mind. See you soon."

Huh. Somebody's playing awfully nice tonight.

"Drive safe."

She arrives forty-five minutes later with an extra-large pizza and an order of meatballs.

"Did you and Sabrina not have lunch?"

"We had salads, but I figured you and I might get hungry again later."

"And here I was worried you might be in a bad mood because you didn't find a chandelier."

"The search continues. I've got time." She slides the pizza box onto the kitchen table and opens it, filling the room with the smell of fresh wood-fired crust and Italian sausage. "I also didn't find the phone I wanted today, but I will."

"What kind of phone?"

"An antique one. Red."

"You mean the kind that hung on the wall and had to be cranked?"

"No, not that old. Did those even come in red? I want one with a dial and a curly cord."

"Hold on." I take a bite of the pizza slice in my hand before I drop it back in the box and walk toward a different kind of box, one I haven't opened in years. But I know exactly where it is.

When I come back into the kitchen with my hand behind my back, she's pouring herself a glass of wine. I wait until she's done and the bottle is back on the table before I bring my hand forward.

"Rhett!"

The happiness in her eyes makes the dust I inhaled digging this thing out totally worth it.

"Is this the kind of phone you're talking about?"

"That is the exact phone! Why do you have that?"

"It was my grandparents'. When we cleaned out their house, one of my cousins said she wanted it and asked me to grab it for her, so I did. Then she changed her mind. I put it in a box with a bunch of other stuff I always meant to go through later. Later never came."

I hold the phone out to her, but she hesitates.

"How did your grandmother have it displayed?"

"She didn't display it. It was their phone that they used every day."

"It looks brand new."

"Their house was always immaculate."

"Even the cord is in perfect condition. It's not stretched out at all."

"It sat on a table between their chairs in the living room. This cord never had to reach far."

"Do you remember them talking on it?"

"Yeah. I might have a picture of my grandmother talking on it somewhere."

"It's so perfect, but I can't take that. It belonged to your grandparents."

"It's not a family heirloom, Twister. It's just an old phone."

"If I take it, I'm going to display it in my new location on Main Street. You sure you want to contribute to that?"

"My grandmother never left the house without touching up her lipstick. She always said a little lipstick might not solve a woman's problems, but it sure wouldn't hurt her any. If I didn't give you this phone, she might haunt me."

"She sounds great."

"Take the phone. My arm's getting sore."

She snatches it from my hand and hugs it to her chest. "I can't believe you had this. You don't happen to have any vintage chandeliers hidden in a barn, do you?"

"That one I can't help with."

"Thank you."

"You're welcome. I've got boxes of other forgotten stuff from their house. I don't remember what all is in them, but I can guarantee it will all be vintage. You're welcome to go through them anytime you want."

"Are you serious? Yes, please!" She sets the phone on the table and picks up her wine—the glass and the bottle. "I want a mix of vintage items from different eras. A retro chic vibe spanning the last century. Forties pin-up art like the postcard, a vintage chandelier, maybe a tufted velvet loveseat. How old do you think the phone is?"

"Probably from the sixties, maybe early seventies."

"It couldn't be any more perfect. I can't wait to see what else you've got."

Before I can turn to show her to the right room, she says, "Bring the pizza."

"I guess I'm going to be of service tonight in a different way than I'd planned."

"The night's young, Daddy. We're just getting started." She brings her wine glass to her lips with a smile.

15

Glynnis

"WAS THIS YOUR GRANDMOTHER'S?" I sit on the floor and hold up the vintage cigarette case I've found. It has a turquoise-colored background with white and black swans facing each other.

Rhett looks down from the twin bed he's sitting on with the pizza box in his lap. "Yeah, her only bad habit, as far as I know."

"It's beautiful. This might be older than the phone, Rhett. It could be worth something."

"If it's worth something to you, it's yours."

I wrap my fingers around it, feeling wrong for wanting it the way I do. But I do want it. I really, really want it.

"I'll display it under glass to be sure no one walks off with it. I was thinking of doing a vignette in a case with a beaded purse, spilling a variety of lipsticks. It would be a great addition to that."

"Take it."

"If you want anything back at any time—"

"I'm not going to want any of it back. If you don't take it, it's getting donated to someone else."

Like hell it is. I add the cigarette case to the pile of trinkets I've already claimed. A compact mirror joins the ranks next.

Rhett genuinely seems to have no attachment to anything I pull from the boxes. He has a funny story for a few of the items, but no signs of sentimentality. Until I find a pipe.

He turns it over in his hands. "Damn, I thought I saved all of his pipes. He collected them."

"He didn't smoke them?"

"Oh, he smoked them, too, but he had some older ones that he just kept on his dresser. My grandmother said as long as he didn't complain about her birds, she wouldn't complain about his pipes."

"She collected birds?"

"Chickadees, specifically. Hundreds of them compared to his half a dozen unsmoked pipes. She thought those little birds were the cutest damn things ever. She had carved chickadees, painted chickadees, little feathered ones. Everywhere. Spent hours of her life dusting those birds."

"The more I hear about her, the more I wish I could've known her."

"She called anyone she loved and had fun with a chickadee, too. All her girlfriends who came over to drink coffee and gossip were chickadees, her grandkids, even when we were being little shitheads. She would've called you one, I'm sure."

"You got rid of all of them, didn't you?"

"Nobody wanted those birds. It might've been the only unanimous decision we made."

"I would've wanted one," I mumble as I start unpacking the next box.

"You need to take a break and eat."

"Don't tell me what to do! Except when I want you to."

"You always want me to tell you what to do."

"Wrong." This box is an odd assortment of stuff that looks like it was probably meant for the trash all along. "Is this the last one?"

"That's it."

"Thank you for letting me go through this stuff."

"Glad you're in the mood to be nice again."

"Sorry. I didn't mean to snap at you. I'm just—"

"Hungry." He cuts me off, but he's right.

"Okay, fine. I'm hungry."

I push the final box of his grandparents' stuff aside and stand up. But when I reach for a slice of pizza, Rhett pulls the box away.

If he thinks I'm going to beg for pizza that I picked up and delivered, he's lost his mind.

He slides over. "Sit."

"Why don't we just take it back into the kitchen?"

"Because there's not a bed in the kitchen."

"I've never known a bed to be a requirement for you."

"It's not a requirement for you either, but I just realized I've never seen you naked in this room."

"This is the first time I've ever been in this room."

"You've been in it for a while now, and yet, you still have clothes on."

"I've been busy. There are several rooms in your house I've never seen."

"So many options. Let's start with this one."

"I'm hungry."

He nods at the space on the bed next to him. "Join me."

His tone deepens even when he gives commands that sound more like suggestions. His whole demeanor shifts. It's subtle, but there is no question mark at the end of his words. My body responds as if his voice has put me into a trance.

That description isn't far off, other than I consciously want to do as he says right now. I'm ready for him to tell me what to do.

"Eat." He brings a slice to my mouth, and my lips part to take a bite. It's good pizza, even at room temperature.

I take the slice from his hand and finish it on my own. He watches me eat, and I swear, before him, the thought of a man watching me eat would've felt about as erotic as the thought of getting a root canal.

But the backs of his fingers are warm against my cheek as they move to tuck my hair behind my ear. I have this annoying layer that's grown just long enough to fall in front of my mouth if I tilt my head in the slightest.

He watches me lick pizza sauce from the corner of my mouth, his smile is faint but smoldering. Our eyes lock. It's not unnerving; it's a form of communication, wordless but powerful.

We both know where this leads, and it's not our eye contact that confirms it.

This feral energy between us shows up organically, never needing to be summoned or coaxed. It heats the moment we acknowledge it with our smiles and our eyes.

He offers me another slice, but I decline it. I may want more later, but right now, I feel warm and cozy. No more hangry inclinations.

"You sure?" he asks.

"I'm sure."

He looks over our shoulders at the iron headboard, and his intentions are as clear as if he's spoken them. The ironwork he's eyeing is designed with thick scrolls and posts . . . the kind that wouldn't bend under the pressure of bound wrists straining against them.

My hips shift, and my inner thighs glide gently against each other as I maneuver my body to sit straighter. Rhett turns his body toward mine, reaching across me for the remote that controls the ceiling fan. With one click, he stops the blades and turns off the light.

The gleam in his eyes is still apparent through the dim light from the lamp on the nightstand. My legs are bare beneath the hem of my shorts, and his hand is warm on my thigh. He squeezes, and it sets off a chain reaction of contractions throughout my body, causing my nipples to harden and my spine to curve.

He rises to his knees and unbuckles his belt. The mattress gives under his weight, but the bed doesn't move or squeak. It's small, but old enough to have been made from good quality materials. Strong and built to last.

I toss the pizza box to the floor, and he raises his eyebrows as if to warn me that was unnecessary.

"The lid was closed," I say. "It's fine."

His belt slides through the denim loops on his jeans with ease. It's worn, but the leather is thick.

"Give me your wrists."

If I toyed with him now, it would ruin the delicious tension that's building, so I comply without hesitation.

He wraps the belt over and under my wrists once, looping it like the infinity symbol, but keeping some slack until he lifts my arms above my head and threads the tail of the belt behind a post, bringing it forward to feed it through the buckle. Pulling it taut, he finds the hole that will fasten it tightly enough that I can't slip free, but not so tight that the leather will dig into my skin.

Not if I hold still.

That's the game, to see how much it takes to make me squirm, to break my resolve and make me writhe with need—whether it's the need for him to stop or the need for more. He won't free me even then, not unless I use a safe word.

He'll keep teasing and testing me until he knows I've taken all I can bear. It happens sooner sometimes than others, but I know he'll sense it before I say it.

When I'm naked from the waist down, and he's pushed my shirt and bra up above my breasts, he looms over me and admires my body while he slowly opens his shirt, one snap at a time, knowing how much I prefer to hear them undone all at once.

My hands fist, driving my fingernails into my palms, but I hold still otherwise, trying to pretend it doesn't bother me at all that he's doing it wrong.

His smile spreads, and I bite mine back. I hate being emotionally or professionally vulnerable. But physically? I spent so long questioning how I could want this with anyone, how I could let myself be so weak, but all it took was one trustworthy man to dispel my internal judgment.

That man opened up so much self-discovery and made it easier to explore with the man who came after him, but I always held back a little, kept my defenses barely paused. In both of those relationships, I felt as safe as I've ever felt with anyone, but there were still limits to how much I could let go.

And then came Rhett, who desires less commitment but inspires more safety. Maybe I feel safer with him precisely because he poses no threat whatsoever to my freedom. Maybe I'm just learning to let go more as I get older.

Maybe he's actually a safer man.

Watching his boxer briefs drop, freeing his familiar hard cock, and seeing his strong hands shove the black fabric down his firm thighs, my wrists pull their leather restraint forward.

I've already lost the ability to hold entirely still. I either have to increase the tension in the belt or let the building tension in my body run free. If I choose the latter, my spine will arch, my hips will rock, and then my legs will bend and straighten until I'm practically undulating beneath him when he hasn't even touched me yet.

And if I let that happen, Rhett's laughter will cascade over me, slow and villainous because he'll think he's won so soon. He knows he's going to win eventually.

We both know.

But for now, I slide my body farther down the mattress, pulling harder on the belt until there's no slack left in my arms. Forcing stillness.

His hands are warm on my forearms. He begins to slide them down to my biceps, over my shoulders, across my bunched shirt and bra, slipping his fingers under to push them up farther before his palms slide to my breasts, squeezing and kneading, letting his thumbs graze my nipples briefly, and then continuing down my ribcage, over my abdomen, my hips and thighs, again letting his thumbs graze against sensitive skin.

When the pads of his thumbs brush against my pussy, my legs attempt to spread, but he holds them between his thighs, only allowing them to part slightly. He holds me there, watching my face for a prolonged moment before his body moves down, freeing my thighs.

He grips one of my ankles and pushes it upward, forcing my leg to bend, bringing it up to rest on his shoulder. His hand roams over my calf to the back of my knee, where his thumb massages circles while his fingers knead above my kneecap.

It relaxes my muscles until my leg is dead weight, entirely under his control.

His mouth is hot on my skin, peppering kisses along my calf before he lifts my other leg and repeats the process.

When he slides down to his forearms, my slack legs slide with him until it's the backs of my knees instead of my feet that rest on his shoulders, my lower legs draping over them.

I can feel the heat of his breath on my tender skin before his lips make contact. The leather bites into my wrists a bit, but I'm not willing to reposition for comfort, wanting to feel the abrasion.

The contrast with the sensation of his soft mouth spawns a tighter clench in my core, but my arousal can't be contained. He moans at the first taste, and his probing tongue instantly releases my clenched walls. The constriction is replaced by fluttering reflexes I couldn't deny if I tried.

Looking down at his satisfied smile, knowing he knows the power he has over me doesn't worry me at all. It feels too good to be known the way he knows me.

I can't remember the thrill of being with someone new anymore, but I can't imagine how it could ever be better than this. My shoulders sink, and the discomfort in my wrists fades until all I can feel is his mouth on me.

Orgasms always leave me sensitive, but as I lie here, breathing through the aftershocks of the one he's just given me, I am hyper-sensitive to the point that his gentle kiss on my swollen clit causes my whole body to convulse.

"You need a minute, huh?"

"I don't want more of that. Just fuck me."

"Hmm, but I had other plans."

"Fine. Bring your dick to my mouth, and then fuck me."

"If I put my dick in your mouth, I'm going to be the one who needs a minute before we can go on."

"Then just fuck me like I so nicely asked."

"I missed the part where you asked nicely."

"Please, Daddy." My voice is breathy and shameless, and it is not at all performative. This isn't role play; it's the most real version of me.

He crawls up my body to kiss my mouth. I roll my hips to encourage him. His erection is heavy between us. With one shift of his hips, he could slide right into me but he doesn't let it happen.

Instead, he looks up at the belt, twisting at a curve in the metal. "Is that hurting you?"

"No. Leave it."

"Let me move you up so it doesn't leave marks on you."

"I don't care if it leaves marks."

"I do."

I relax my arms as he helps me slide up closer to the headboard. If he's worried about the leather leaving marks on my wrists, he won't be able to fuck me the way I want. As far as I'm concerned, if there are marks, I can wear heavy bangles for a few days. I always wear bracelets; no one would bat an eye. But I don't want him to hold back.

I do what he wants so he'll do what I want—the way we both like it.

16

Rhett

S OMETIMES, WE KEEP THINGS for reasons we can't see yet, and I guess maybe I kept these boxes so Glynnis could go through them yesterday. But now that she's had a chance to take what she wants from them, it's long past time to donate what's left.

I lift a box to carry it to my truck and immediately see the things she saved still clustered in a small pile on the rug.

"Shit." I shake my head, staring down at them.

She'll be in town for a while, but I want to take these things to her today. Any excuse to see her. But also, knowing her, she's probably keeping a running inventory of everything she's gathering, and I don't want her to go looking for this stuff and think she's lost it.

Eldon Roundtree drives past and waves as I'm pulling out of the thrift store parking lot. I wave at him, but it's out of reflex more than friendliness.

His colleagues are taking their sweet time rendering an opinion on whether or not Twister's attorney misinterpreted the restrictions. In other words, delaying admitting their screw up.

Nothing pisses me off more than people refusing to honor their word or not owning up to a mistake.

What's done is done with her purchase, I know that. But if we can firm up our intentions going forward, the sooner the better in my opinion. Clearly, not everyone in this town feels obliged to disclose their intent to sell, regardless of what they agreed to in the past.

There could be another pending sale on Main Street at any minute. People didn't used to be so damn secretive. But now, you can't assume anybody's being honest about their intentions.

I know I should've called her before I headed for the cabin, but I'm already almost there. No point in calling now. It's not like I'm dropping in, expecting to stay. With any luck, Sabrina won't see my truck coming up the driveway. She's the one I should really be worried about. Never mind that they spent all afternoon together yesterday.

Sabrina definitely sees me. She couldn't miss me, seeing as how she and Glynnis are both standing in front of the cabin.

And there's a suitcase on the ground between them.

"You leaving so soon?" I ask as I step out of my truck, half-joking, telling myself there's another reason for that suitcase. It probably has stuff for the spa. She said she was staying for a few weeks, and she's barely been here a few days.

"What are you doing here?" she asks.

"I came to bring you these." I hold out the clear plastic bag that contains her finds from the boxes. "Found them on the rug earlier."

"Oh, damn. Thank you. I would've freaked out if I started looking for them and couldn't find them."

"I know. That's why I brought them over." I hand her the bag. "What's with the suitcase?"

Sabrina ducks her head and walks off toward the house without a word. Not a hello, goodbye, kiss my ass, nothing. My gut twists.

"I was just about to put it in the car." She tilts the suitcase and pulls it along by the handle toward her rental car, as if that answers my question.

I grab her arm. "You're leaving?"

"My general contractor says it'll take several weeks to get permits. Unless you can pull some strings to make that happen faster, there's no reason for me to be here. I'll come back once they get started."

"No reason to be here, huh? No reason to let me know you were leaving either?"

"Can you speed up the permit process, Rhett?"

"Nope, can't say that I can. Were you going to call me? Stop on the way out of town to say goodbye?"

"I don't live here. I always leave."

"You don't usually sneak away, though. How'd you see this going if I hadn't come over and caught you leaving?"

"Caught me? I'm free to come and go from this place whenever I want."

"Yeah, you're right. You are." I turn away from her and walk toward my truck.

"It's not like I'm fleeing the country. Why are you acting like this?"

I spin around, ready to fucking rip a tree up by its roots. "Did you just assume Mav would let me know?"

She shrugs. "Maybe. Or we'd talk later today, and I'd let you know then."

"You flew in. You had to change your flight. This wasn't a spontaneous decision to drive home. When did you decide to leave?"

"What difference does that make?"

"Did you know yesterday? Had you already decided? Is that why you didn't stay the night?"

"We don't always stay the night with each other. We used to never do that."

"But now we do more often than we don't. Did you know when you came over yesterday that you were leaving today?"

"Yes. I knew."

"Why didn't you tell me?"

"I don't know. It felt pointless to bring it up."

"Pointless. Okay."

I change direction and walk toward the house.

"Where are you going?"

"To visit with friends."

"You never show up unannounced to hang out."

"Didn't do that today either. I came over to give you something. I gave it to you. And since I'm here, I'm going to hang out. Don't you have a plane to catch? Don't let me keep you."

"You're being ridiculous. You better not go in there thinking you're going to talk shit about me because you know Sabrina won't stand for it."

"I don't anticipate your name coming up at all. Safe travels."

"Fine," she says. "Enjoy your visit."

"Enjoy your flight."

Her car door slams as I take the first step up to Mav and Sabrina's porch. When my knuckles meet the wood, her tires are already kicking up dust, heading down the long driveway toward the road that will lead her out of Grinberry Falls.

Sabrina meets my eyes when I walk in. "It's not you that she's running from, Rhett."

"I'm not really in the mood for a psychoanalytical breakdown of the situation."

Mav offers a beer, and I take it.

"Okay," Sabrina says, standing from the couch. "But if you decide you want to talk about it later, let me know."

"I never figured you'd be one to betray her confidence," I say.

"I'm not. But I can explain some things in general terms that might keep you from being so pissed off."

"I'll keep that in mind. But right now, I'm gonna drink this beer and be pissed off."

"Knock yourself out." She walks into the kitchen.

Mav shakes his head. "I only have one thing to say."

"Choose wisely."

"You are two of the most hardheaded people I know, and honestly, I'm surprised y'all made it as long as you did."

"Did I say I didn't want to see her again? Did you hear her say she didn't want to see me again? No. So maybe cool it on the whole being surprised we made it as long as we did bullshit."

"Oh."

His smirk pisses me off more than I already am. You'd think he'd be able to read my expression, but no, he just keeps running his mouth.

"Okay, you're aware that one of you is going to have to give in and start a conversation about this, right?"

"About what exactly?"

"The fact that you're not just casually seeing each other whenever it's convenient anymore."

"I thought you only had one thing to say."

"You asked me a question."

"Fuck you."

He turns up the TV, but that damn smirk on his face is louder.

17

Glynnis

Enzo has walked all his subcontractors through my little blue house to take measurements and talk about the new layout. We've gone back and forth on a few sketches. It's been enough to keep my mind occupied for a few days. Part of the time, anyway.

Aside from a text asking if I made it home, Rhett hasn't reached out. I responded. I'm not that petty. But I guess we had nothing else to say to each other because neither one of us initiated a conversation beyond confirming my safety.

Sabrina says he was pissed off and didn't want to talk when he came into the house after I left. She didn't come right out and say it, but I know she thinks he has a right to be mad.

I'm sure Mav is totally on his side. Not that anybody needs to pick a side. It's really not that big a deal.

I didn't need anybody's permission to come home. If I've ruined things between us by not updating him on my whereabouts every second of the day, he obviously never knew me at all.

Except he did know me. Does know me.

Maybe I didn't know him as well as I thought, though.

Except I absolutely knew he'd try to talk me into staying, which is exactly why I didn't tell him I was leaving. And I knew he'd be mad when he found out I'd left without saying goodbye, but I also knew there was a damn good chance I'd give in and stay if he asked me to.

Getting that comfortable with someone who lives two states away is a bad idea.

The plastic bag of treasures he let me take from his grandparents' things keeps taunting me from my bar where I flung it when I pulled it out of my purse. I was frantically trying to find my phone but shouldn't have been so careless with those things.

I carefully open the bag and pull out the compact, pausing to take a breath and hope it's intact before I open it.

It's perfect, not a single crack. Damn, I got lucky. I check the cigarette case next. The enamel's fine, again no cracks other than the slight crazing on the surface that was already there. No damage to the hinges. I open and close it a few times just to be sure.

My body is tired—not muscle-strain exhaustion, but stress fatigue. It's not a new feeling, but I've done a good job of keeping it at bay with yoga and meditation for a while. I could do one of those things now, but I don't want to.

I want a hot bath. And a glass of wine.

Sinking down until the base of my neck meets the back of the tub, I take a sip of wine and watch ribbons of steam rise from the water's surface. I set my glass on the teak tray that spans the width of the bathtub, exchanging it for my phone.

All the woo-woo influencers—and my therapist—say "Put down your phone if you want to relax." I can relax just fine with my phone in my hand, thanks.

I scroll through postings for upcoming local estate sales, searching for a vintage settee or loveseat. The moment I attempt to click on an image for more information, a call comes in, causing the listing to vanish.

Dammit.

It's a video call.

His favorite kind when I'm here and he's there. My pulse quickens at the sight of his face on my screen. So much for being just fine not talking to him.

I answer. "Hey."

"Sweet Jesus. I had no idea my timing would be so good."

"Unlike mine?"

"I didn't call to argue, Twister."

"That's really not why you called, or you just changed your mind when you realized I was naked?"

"That's really not why I called. Besides, all I can see is from your shoulders up."

"But you can tell I'm in the tub."

"Yeah. That was the reason for the sweet Jesus comment."

"What are you doing?" I ask, hoping to redirect the conversation before his voice lowers.

"Just got back from a committee meeting."

"Did you have everyone throw darts at my picture?"

"Hell, no. It wasn't amateur hour. We used flaming arrows."

"Hope you didn't burn down city hall on my account."

"Not yet. It got a little heated, but nobody had to call the fire department. Speaking of heated, that looks like a hot bath."

"The only kind I take. And if you know what's good for you, you'll hold your next request."

"Not feeling inclined to obey tonight, huh?"

Not as far as I'm willing to let you know.

"Feels a little presumptuous, given the way we left things."

"I miss you, Twister. That's why I called. And if that's not something you want to hear, too bad. It's true, and not saying it doesn't make it go away. I'm still pissed about the way you left, but I fucking miss you."

"You don't get to just say things like that, Rhett. You can't—"

"The hell I can't! I can say whatever the fuck I need to say. You don't miss me? Fine. Say it. Say it to my face. Tell me you don't miss me when you leave here."

"Of course, I fucking miss your stubborn ass! But that doesn't change anything between us."

"Why is that?"

"Because it can't, Rhett."

"According to who?"

"Us! We said we weren't going to do this."

"No, we actually didn't." He sighs. "Maybe we both felt the same about not wanting any strings in the beginning, but there were never any spoken rules about where this could go. We probably both assumed it wasn't going to go anywhere, but goddammit, Twister! It's going somewhere for me."

"I knew you were going to fuck up my life the moment I met you."

"All you knew the moment you met me was that you wanted to unsnap my shirt."

"And all you knew was that you wanted to see your handprint on my ass."

"That's not true. I wanted to see your tits, too. They look amazing right now, by the way."

I look down. Apparently, at some point during all this reminiscing, I've sat straight up in my tub. In my defense, it's hard to yell effectively when your chin is tucked.

"You could've told me I was yelling at you with my tits out."

"Be serious."

"Okay, so we miss each other when we're apart," I say, refusing to smile at his comment. "What are we supposed to do about that? We live apart. That's just reality."

"We could be apart less. My schedule's clear for the next couple of days. I could come to Scottsdale."

"Really? You'd do that?"

"I've been there before. It's just been a while because we were both trying so damn hard to pretend we didn't need to see each other. But I don't want to pretend anymore. I need to see you."

"What about Bo? Don't you need time to make arrangements for him?"

"Joni's always happy to watch him. He likes her place. It's like his vacation home."

"So, get on a plane, Daddy. What are you waiting for?"

"Stay in that tub until I get there."

We both laugh, but deep down, there is a part of me that wants to scream. At him. At myself. What are we doing?

But then again, what choice do we have? It's time to try or quit. Holding out in the gray area in between isn't working anymore.

We end the call, and I finish my wine, letting anticipation turn to fear, then to hope and back to fear again. The water's cold by the time I convince myself to get out of the tub.

No matter who I try to make him out to be in my fears, the truth comes through: he's a good guy. If I'd been looking for any kind of guy when we met, it would've been a bad one, one I could easily walk away from because he was no good to begin with. One who was here for a good time, but not a long time.

That's who I thought Rhett was: not necessarily a bad guy, but a temporary one. And now he wants to stick around. And I want him around.

And I don't know what to do with any of this. I guess I just let it happen?

18

Rhett

I SEND HER A message to let her know my plane just landed. She sends back three heart emojis, which I assume means she's here, or will be by the time I walk outside. Whatever happened to using words? Now, we're all supposed to be able to interpret symbols and cartoon faces.

I'm not mad at the hearts. I just object to them on general principles.

Watching her silver Mercedes enter the pickup line makes me smile. She loves that damn car. I walk down the sidewalk to meet her.

If she'd cut it any closer whipping between cars to get to the inside lane, her beloved car would be wearing a new Volkswagen as a hood ornament. She barely has it in park before she hops out and runs around to hug me hello.

The feel of her in my arms eases my agitation. Her hair smells fresh, and the scent of her perfume, though faint through the exhaust fumes of idling cars, makes me pull her closer to smell it for one more moment before the traffic officer waves his little orange baton and tells us this is a no parking zone.

"You can drive," she says.

"I thought that was a given."

"Don't make me change my mind."

I jump in front of her to open her passenger door before she can reach for it.

"Thanks," she says with a barely noticeable eyeroll.

Chivalry bothers her. She's gotten better about it, but no matter how many times I explain that I don't open doors for her because I think she's incapable, her eyes continue to mock the concept. I'm going to keep opening doors for her. If she wants to strain her eyes over it, that's her business.

My agitation ramps up again as I drive. I complain about the lack of grass and real trees, the traffic, construction everywhere you look . . . things that exist all over Texas, too, not even that far from Grinberry Falls.

Congestion aggravates me in Texas, but today, it instantly aggravates me more in Arizona. Everything about this state aggravates me.

"This place is a fucking hellscape." I wave my hand at the windshield, gesturing to the sign we're passing under. "Dust storm warning. Why do you live here again?"

"Because I love it. I love the desert and the mountains and every modern amenity in between that pisses you off. Take the next exit. We're going to brunch. You need to eat."

"I hate the whole idea of brunch, from its stupid name to the ridiculous shit on the menu."

"Are you hungry?"

"Yes."

"It's ten a.m. We're going to brunch, and I'm going to moan in ecstasy while I eat avocado toast with micro greens and pumpkin seeds and goat cheese."

"Nobody will be able to hear you over the champagne-drunk women, complaining about their pampered lives in whatever fancy-ass restaurant we're headed for."

"Sometimes, you have no idea what you're talking about. This is about to be one of those times. Turn left at the light."

The parking lot is crowded. Strike one.

The coffee options all have cutesy names like "Red-Eye Bulls-eye (espresso)" and "Wake Me up Before You No-Show (de-caf)." It takes me five minutes to find plain black coffee, which I refuse to order as a "Workaday Joe." Strike two.

The menu has avocado toast, a tofu scramble, a protein bowl with ground turkey, black beans, and quinoa . . . but the other side offers a steak and eggs platter with thick-cut bacon and home fries, buttermilk biscuits with sausage gravy, and a triple-meat omelet.

Well, damn. She found a place with a brunch menu that has actual food on it. And the ridiculous names only infect the drinks. No strike three.

I order the steak and eggs. She orders her avocado toast and a "Jessica Rabbit," which she explains is just a blend of chili peppers, passion fruit, and carrot juice.

"No mimosa?"

"Not unless you want me to fall asleep as soon as we get back in the car."

"You didn't sleep well last night?"

"No," she admits. "Did you?"

"Not really."

After brunch, we head for her place, and I don't bitch about the Slingshots whizzing between cars or the fact that there's a Starbucks at every exit. We need to have what might be our first serious conversation about us, and I need to be even-keeled for it.

We've had serious conversations about the world at large, and shared personal stories with each other, but the only use of "us" meant people in general, not her-plus-me us.

She slides down in the passenger seat, her eyelids heavy, the sun making the highlights in her hair sparkle and warming her cheeks. I don't think abstaining from champagne is going to keep her awake much longer. Maybe we'll nap and then talk.

Her condo is a two-story corner unit, so she only has an attached neighbor on one side. Still one side too many if you ask me. The grounds are covered in rocks and cactus, no grass, but there are a few real trees—not big ones, but they're trees.

It suits her lifestyle, easy to lock and leave whenever she wants. No yard to maintain, and there's onsite maintenance. I couldn't live this way, but I understand why it works for her.

I take her hand after she closes the front door behind us. "You think maybe we should talk?"

My gut knots when she doesn't answer right away, but then she nods.

"I was thinking about saying we should take a nap first," she says. "But I don't really think that will make it any easier."

"It doesn't have to be hard."

She nods again and pulls on my hand to bring me with her to the couch.

I sit on the end cushion, and she sits in the middle with her legs pulled up, facing me.

"So, I guess we're doing this, huh?" Her shoulders lift as if she's not positive what I meant last night.

"Define what you mean by *this*," I say.

"This." Her hand swings between us. "You and me."

"Us," I clarify.

"Yeah. You and me being an official us."

"I hope that's what we're doing," I search her eyes, trying to determine where she's at emotionally.

"Okay. Yeah. I'm in."

Her tone is flat, and I was definitely hoping for more enthusiasm. "I'm not asking you to join a committee. I'm asking if you're ready to try a long-distance relationship. A real one."

"I'm ready. I just wish I knew what that was going to look like for us in the long run, you know?"

"I don't have a crystal ball, but I'd bet on us before I'd put money on anybody else."

"That's the thing, though," she says. "It's a gamble."

"Life's a fucking gamble. Moving away from home to go to college in another state was a gamble. Moving to another new state after graduation was a gamble. Opening a business is a gamble. You're not afraid of taking risks."

"If those things hadn't worked out, my heart wouldn't have been broken."

"Yes, it would have."

She stares at me like she's astonished by my response.

"I love my business, Rhett, but it's not a person. It's different to fail a person."

"I'm the one who's divorced, remember? You don't have to warn me what it's like when it doesn't work out with someone. But I don't think of my divorce as a failure. We were both too young. We grew apart. It didn't work out in the end, but not because we failed each other. And you and I are both a hell of a lot more established and mature than she and I were. Is the fact that I'm so much older than you a concern?"

"No. You're only forty-four."

"And you're only thirty-two."

"I've always preferred older men. You know this about me."

"Well, something's eating at you. Do you not feel the same way I do?"

"I think I do."

"You think?"

"I'm not sure how you feel. You said you miss me and this is turning into something and you could come to Scottsdale and—"

"I love you. Does that clear things up?"

"Wow. You just said that so easily."

"I didn't come to it easy. Maybe that's what I should have said last night instead of I miss you. I miss you because I love you. I'm sorry I didn't say that to begin with."

"I'm glad you said it in person instead."

"And?"

A tear wells in the corner of her eye, and I really need her to say something right now.

"Is it okay if I'm scared to love you?"

"Why are you scared to fall in love with me?"

"No, that would be a past tense fear. I'm already in love with you. It just scares the shit out of me."

"You can't control it. That's why it scares you."

"Yeah, exactly."

"Have you ever been able to control falling in love with someone?"

"No," she says softly. "But I've never fallen this hard. I at least felt like I could control that much before you."

"Nobody can control any of it. It just happens."

"It didn't just happen." She wipes the tear that's finally fallen. "It happened because you spent two years giving me space and making me laugh and sitting with me on the banks of a creek just letting me breathe and knowing exactly what I need all the goddamn time and . . ."

Her breathing gets shallow as she fights back tears. I want her to open up, but I can't stand to see her cry. I move closer and put my hands on her shoulders, looking directly into her eyes.

"Hey, look at me. You deserve someone who does all those things. Hell, you deserve so much more. But that's too bad because you already fell in love with me."

"Well, yeah, after you tricked me into it."

"For what it's worth, I could make a list of all the sneaky things you did to trick me, too."

"Pfft. Please. My magic's way too powerful for you to comprehend."

"I comprehend you just fine."

"Quit trying to scare me."

"Let's take a nap."

I T'S AMAZING HOW FAST two days can fly by. I feel like I just got here, but we're back at her decent brunch spot before she drops me off for my flight home. I'd stay longer if I could.

My "Workaday Joe" just got refilled, and her "Jessica Rabbit" is half gone when she looks up from her quinoa bowl and says, "Thank you for coming to the cabin that morning to bring me the things I'd left at your house. They mean more to me than you know."

"I'm glad they're with someone who can appreciate them. And if I hadn't brought them over, we might not be sitting here right now."

"You wouldn't have been mad at me if you'd found out I was gone after I'd already left?"

"I'd have been mad, but getting angry face-to-face makes a difference. It was in the moment, no time for me to cool off about it."

She laughs, and her gray-blue eyes shine.

"Thank you for telling me those personal things about your grandmother, too. Especially her comment about how a little lipstick wouldn't hurt a woman. Sometimes, that gets said in a judgmental way, telling a woman she'd look better if she bothered to put on makeup, but I like the way your grandmother used it. She made it sound empowering. It reminded me of a neighbor who meant a lot to me when I was growing up."

"You've never mentioned this neighbor. Was she like a grand-mother to you?"

"No, Grace was too young to be a grandmother. She was a mom, but her kids were way younger than me. She'd always let me hang out with her. I thought she was beautiful and so cool. She never forced me to talk about anything going on at home, but she'd always make me feel better by saying, 'I bet a little lipstick wouldn't hurt.' And then she'd let me try on all her makeup. None of it was high-end, but it was the best she could afford, and she knew that cheap lipstick would make me feel special. I'd have to wash it off before I went home, but it was worth it."

"Sounds like she cared about you."

"She was the only adult who actually paid attention to me. Positive attention. At a time when I really needed it. She didn't have to let a hurt little girl rummage through her makeup. If I'd broken something, she probably couldn't have afforded to replace it until payday, or for a few paydays, but she always offered. I know now that she knew if I was occupied with something that made me happy, she could get me to talk. All I knew then was that she was safe and kind and fun."

"Grace sounds pretty amazing."

"When I graduated, she gave me a gift bag full of drugstore makeup and a twenty-dollar bill that I'm pretty sure she couldn't really afford to give away. But I needed it, the money and the lip-stick. It wasn't just makeup; it was a reminder that I could survive hard times."

"Does Grace know how you're doing now?"

"I've sent her every new product since day one. And I make sure she gets a signature kit a few times a year. Her girls, too."

"I bet she's proud of you."

"I'm proud of her. She makes a difference in a world where not everyone bothers."

"Yeah, I was right."

"About what?"

"My grandmother definitely would've called you a chickadee."

She smiles, and I want to reschedule my flight. But I've got to get used to leaving when I want to stay. And trusting that we're good even when we're apart.

19

Glynnis

PULLING UP TO MY little blue house and seeing permits finally posted in the front window dissolves the exhaustion
from my drive. Hammers start swinging tomorrow. Tonight,
Main Street is quiet. The only places still open are Trudy's
Diner and Grin's Pub.

I park in front of my diamond in the rough and walk next
door to meet Rhett for a late dinner. Oliver's owner, Joni, is
walking out as I'm walking in.

"Looks like things are about to start happening next door,"
she says as she hugs me hello. Joni's a hugger.

"Tomorrow. I can't believe how long it's taken to get permits."

"Well, welcome to Grinberry Falls. I'm happy for you. Looking forward to the grand opening."

"You and me both. Hey, thanks for taking Bo again last week so Rhett could come see me. I know you've had him quite a few times over the past few months."

"I love that ridiculous dog. If I'm home, he's always welcome. Do you know if your general contractor does residential projects? I think I'm about ready to remodel my money pit of a house."

"He does. I'll send you his information."

"Great. Enjoy your dinner."

"Thanks, Joni. Wait. Where's Oliver?" I see his trailer hooked to her truck, but I haven't seen him prancing down the sidewalk yet.

We both look up the street just in time to see Mav opening the door of Grin's Pub to let the alpaca out.

"Looks like he was having a drink while I picked up dinner," Joni says.

"Just another night in Grinberry Falls." I laugh and walk inside while she opens the trailer for her prince of an alpaca.

I slide into the booth to sit across from Rhett. "Did you see those beautiful permits gleaming in my front window?"

"I did. I've also heard quite a bit about them." He turns his tea glass a quarter turn, his eyes following the shifting ice cubes.

"What does that mean?"

He looks up, and I know instantly that I don't want to hear what he's about to say.

"There was a group of women at last night's city council meeting . . . a small, but very vocal group. They live in that new subdivision with the big water fountain at the entrance. Not actual locals, but they've been here for five minutes, so they think they are. Anyway, their complaint boils down to the claim that they bought houses in Grinberry Falls based on the small-town charm, and they don't think Sugar Lips fits on Main Street."

I laugh at the audacity. "What do they think I'm going to do, stop the whole project because they disapprove? If they don't like Sugar Lips, they don't have to walk inside. No one is going to force them to become customers."

"The irony is that they look like they'd be your ideal customers."

"Oh, please. Some bored housewives, who probably sit around judging other women's choices because they're too scared to make their own and too uninformed to have anything else to talk about? Those women are not the ideal Sugar Lips customers. Do you know their names?"

"I don't, but it's public record. Although I think ignoring them is probably the wisest choice."

"I know. I'd just like to know who they are when they call to schedule a party or come in to make a purchase. They'll bitch to anyone who'll listen before they know anything about it, but then they'll come in and pretend they've loved it all along. Because women like that can't stand to be left out of anything. There are real atrocities happening in the world that they could be speaking out against, but they don't actually have convictions; they just have loud mouths and an insatiable desire for attention."

"You're not worried about bad word-of-mouth exposure in the meantime?"

"It's not even open yet. What are they going to bad-mouth? Aside from the fact that they don't think it fits, whatever that means. I know for a fact there are people in this town who don't think the houses those women live in fit here, but nobody is stopping them from living in them."

"To be fair, some of us did try."

"Some of you already tried to keep Sugar Lips out, too. It didn't work, and if those women think they've got a shot at it, they're delusional. There's already a nail salon on Main Street. Why wouldn't a lip spa fit?"

"I just told you so you can be prepared."

"Thanks. But those are the type of women who buy big expensive houses in neighborhoods with strict HOAs for the sake of appearances and then get mad when a neighbor turns them in for having backyard chickens that they only got in the first place because some trad-wife influencer made them believe they were scooping chicken shit for Jesus. They are all for restrictions until they're the ones being restricted."

"I never knew you had such strong feelings about chickens."

"I think anyone who genuinely wants to raise chickens should be free to do that. I also think women who live-stream performative homesteading bullshit from the butler's pantry in their 4000-square-foot house while they get rich selling organic chicken supplements to their followers are hypocrites who deserve to be called out. Be who you are, but be for real. That's what I have strong feelings about."

"No one can ever say you lack passion."

"I mean, they could say it, but they'd be wrong."

Merilee comes over to take our order. I'm so glad her mom's diner is going to be my neighbor. Her smiling face always brightens my day. I love her because she's sweet but can be salty when she needs to, just like her mom. It worries me that she doesn't seem to have much of a social life. Probably because all she does is work. Between being a nurse and waitressing part-time . . .

Oh, my gosh! I bet she and Enzo would be perfect together. They're probably about the same age. Both attractive, hard-working, and smart. He's going to be around constantly for the next couple of months.

First, I'll get to know him better to be sure they're a good fit, and then I'll make sure they get to know each other.

Operation matchmaker is about to begin.

"Why are you smiling like that?" Rhett asks.

"Just excited to see my project get started."

Both of them.

"After we eat, do you want to walk through your little blue house one last time before walls start coming down?"

"Walk through it, or christen it with some filthy act that should only be committed behind the privacy of walls?"

"Lady's choice."

"Tempting me with a good time so early in the night?"

"Since when do we do things by the clock?"

When we open the back door and step into the dark kitchen, it feels like we're sneaking into someplace we shouldn't be. Rhett flips the light switch, and I toss my purse onto the chipped tiles of the counter, taking a good hard look at the way the room looks now before everything changes.

"I own this place." Damn, that feels good to say.

Rhett's hands grip my hips from behind. He steps in close enough for his beard to prickle my cheek as he slides one hand between my legs and squeezes me there.

"Who owns this?"

"It's all yours, Daddy."

His shoulders shudder, and I smile. Every now and then, his control slips. Knowing I can do that to him makes me feel . . . not powerful, necessarily, but powerfully connected to him.

It hits me like light flooding a dark room that I'm not afraid to feel that way anymore. It always felt a little good, but it came with a pang of discomfort. Right now, the connection feels entirely good.

He walks me into the darkness of the front room. The bright light from the kitchen fades within a few feet, but there is still too much visibility.

"That window is completely uncovered," I say. "And you are completely wrong if you think you're taking my pants off in front of it."

His hand kneads my pussy through my thin sweatpants.

I dressed for comfort to make the drive, but these pants are also easy-on-easy-off, which is why he loves them.

"Seems like I should be able to expose what's mine where and when I want."

He knows better. "Red light."

"Awwwww," he groans, but he redirects us toward the hallway, stopping after a single step around the corner. The glow of headlights bathes the front window as someone pulls into a parking space out front.

I breathe a sigh of relief that I safe-worded us out of the direct line of sight. This town is clearly going to give me enough grief without literally catching me with my pants down.

I've no sooner thought those words than Rhett yanks my pants to my knees, taking my underwear with them, baring my ass in a hallway that will be walked by workers again and again tomorrow as they move from room to room, making final decisions, swinging hammers, and removing demolition debris.

The voices from the sidewalk float back to us as people get out of the car at the exact moment that Rhett's firm hand strikes my ass.

I know the people outside can't hear the slap, but being able to hear their words carried on the night air makes them feel closer than they are—close enough that if they took a step in our direction, turned their heads our way . . .

He pulls my shirt over my head and drops it to the floor. My bra falls next, leaving me naked for all intents and purposes before he spanks again.

I'm all his, and he's provided just enough cover that I'll allow him full access. Mostly free rein.

We'll never be able to do this again in this exact spot. It won't exist after tonight. I close my eyes, but rather than shut out the workers moving past us in my mind and the onlookers peering around the corner, I see them, seeing me.

I feel the sting and the redness rising on my skin as my arousal slickens my inner thighs.

The darkness of the hallway intensifies the heat. The people from the car are out of earshot now, probably already inside Trudy's, but I can feel eyes on me still. And the warmth of his hand soothing the sting, squeezing, sliding between my legs. Slip-sliding in the mess he's already caused.

"Tell me again who this pussy belongs to."

"You, Daddy. It belongs to you."

My eyes flutter open, and when they close again, walls fall, light blooms, and everyone else disappears.

20
Rhett

S HE'S ONLY BEEN GONE for three days, but after having her here for two weeks, it feels like so much longer. We used to go months between seeing each other, but that feels like another lifetime now.

I back into a spot in front of the boutique next to her little blue house, pretend I'm not checking up on the contractors as I walk down the sidewalk to Trudy's. The demolition is complete and cleared out. Framing is up for the new layout, and a crew is installing ductwork for her new central air and heat system.

Her general contractor hops out of his truck and waves. He's on the phone, but I'm sure Enzo knows I'm checking up on his guys. That's why he got out of his truck, to make sure there isn't a problem.

I wave at him and keep walking as if I'm just passing by on my way to lunch. Still think he seems too young to be a GC, but I'm not here to interfere, just observing.

Mav and Sabrina are seated in a booth in Trudy's, passing a phone back and forth to each other. She looks at the screen with her eyes wide and her mouth moving a mile a minute. He looks at her like she's speaking a language he doesn't understand.

Not sure I want to interrupt whatever's going on there.

Too late. Sabrina sees me and motions me over.

Why do I have the feeling I'm about to be asked for an opinion I don't want to give? It's not like I can get out of it now.

"Good," Mav says, looking up at me. "My wife wants to immortalize Grinberry Falls in another film, but this time, she wants to use our house!"

"No, that's not true," Sabrina says. "Just the driveway and the exterior. And the cows in the pasture. It wouldn't even be the main setting. A couple of scenes, that's it."

I run my fingers through my hair. "Well, unless y'all have purchased some cattle I'm not aware of, Mav doesn't own those cows in your pastures, so he can't authorize having them appear in a movie."

Her face lights up. "Your house sits pretty far in on your property, too. And you have cows in pastures, too."

"I don't own the cows grazing on my land either."

"Well, just give me a name, and I'll negotiate with the cows' owner for that part. Mav objects to having our house shown at all. As if someone will stalk our front porch. It's literally just a few scenes. Wouldn't you like to get paid to have a couple of scenes filmed on your property?"

"No. Sorry. Not interested."

Joni shows up, her voice breezy as she interrupts us. "This looks like a serious meeting for lunch."

Before Mav or I can speak, Sabrina gives her version of how he and I are both being unreasonable.

Without flinching, Joni says, "I have land. Not as much as y'all, and no cows, but if the production company wants to lease some and bring them out for the shoots, I'd be fine with it. And if they just want a long driveway and the outside of an old house in the scenes, I've definitely got those."

"Are you serious?" Sabrina asks.

"Sure. Why not?"

Sabrina glares at Mav, and then at me, before she thanks Joni and tells her she'll ride out to her place later to talk specifics.

"Swing by whenever," Joni says. "I'm picking up a to-go order, and then I'll be around the house for the rest of the day." She says her goodbyes and walks away.

Now that we can eat in peace, I slide in next to Sabrina to join her and Mav for lunch.

She looks right at me and says, "I'm telling your girlfriend you were mean to me today."

"She'll probably be glad for the opportunity to yell at me. I've been on my best behavior for a while now."

"If she wanted to yell at you, she'd just do it."

"Finally. Something we agree on."

We all nod, laugh, and place our orders.

T WISTER'S PROTEST CLUB IS back for another city council meeting appearance. Funny how they somehow only
show up when she's not in town.

Eldon Roundtree caught up with me at Grin's before we all
drove over for the meeting and confirmed that our restrictions
were indeed not airtight. They'll be rewritten, but Sugar Lips
is a go, and there is nothing anyone can do about it.

But that doesn't stop these three women from stepping up
to the mic to state their objections again. The city council has
to let them speak, so we all have to sit through it.

The one with the bright pink fingernails seems to be their
leader. The other two do a lot of nodding and saying, "yeah"
and "exactly" when she speaks.

Pink Fingernails steps away from the mic but decides she's
not done after all. She steps forward again, and her eyes sweep
menacingly over the seated council members as she says, "Oh,
and just in case y'all didn't know, the owner of Sugar Lips is
a felon. Good luck to everyone who's ready to roll out the red
carpet and give her a warm welcome. I guess I just didn't realize
things like that happened in a place like Grinberry Falls."

I'm on my feet, blocking her path by the time she turns
around.

"Things like what?" I demand. "Tell me exactly what it is
you think she's done in this town that anyone should have a
problem with."

"Security!" she yells like she's being robbed in a department store.

I stand my ground, still a good five feet away from her and shirk Mav's hand off my shoulder.

"Name one thing she's done to cause a problem in Grinberry Falls."

"Trust me, I'm keeping an eye on her," she says.

"Is that right? Where is she right now?"

She rolls her eyes and huffs. "I don't answer to you."

I step aside to let her walk past, not realizing Sabrina came in late and took a seat in the back. She never comes to these meetings, but I know by the look in her eyes as she stomps toward Pink Fingernails that she's about to make her presence incredibly well-known.

I'm definitely not the one Mav should be worried about.

"First of all!" Sabrina shouts in the smug woman's face. "You don't even know Glynnis Ramsey. Second of all, your nosey ass can get—"

Mav spins her around to face him instead. "Let it go, Brina," he says in a calm voice that is destined to piss her off more than she already is.

She struggles to break past him.

Pink Fingernails gathers her purse from her seat, and she and her two friends scurry out the side door with their backs hunched like they're fleeing an angry mob throwing rocks at their heads.

If Sabrina had a rock to throw, I doubt she'd miss, so their posture is probably not a bad idea.

We take the three seats the women have vacated so Mav and I can sit on either side of Sabrina. She's consumed with rage. Nobody who knows her would be shocked if she bolted in pursuit.

When the meeting's adjourned, we walk to the parking lot to-gether. A few people try to stop and talk, but Mav waves them off. Sabrina's still wound up like an eight-day clock.

I stand next to Mav's truck in the parking lot, leaning in the window to talk to them. Sabrina's fuming in the passenger seat, but I have to know.

"Does she really have a felony?"

She turns her face toward me like she's never heard such a boring question. "Pffft … class 4, practically a misdemeanor. No jail time. She wasn't the only damn college student on probation."

"What did she do?"

"Got a lawyer, served her probation, and went on with her life."

"You know I'm asking what she did to warrant the felony."

"What makes you think it was warranted? People get charged with things they didn't do every day in this country."

"What is it that she may or may not have done?"

"I'm not telling you her business. Ask her yourself if you want to know."

"Okay. I'll do that. Of course, I'm sure you'll have already texted her to let her know I'm going to ask before I even make it to my truck."

"Stop flinging accusations at me."

"I'll wait until I get to the house to call her. That should give you plenty of time to fill her in on everything."

Mav smiles at me as he puts his truck in reverse. I take my time walking to my truck, replaying that whole scene from the meeting in my head. What the hell does that woman have against Glynnis?

And what the hell did Twister do to catch a felony?

21
Glynnis

B RINA TRIES TO BREAK the news to me gently, but she's so bad at pretending there aren't words burning the back of her tongue while she tries to make small talk, which she's also bad at. Besides, we're best friends; we don't do small talk.

"Tell me whatever it is you actually called to tell me."

"Fuck. Okay. I kept having this nagging feeling that I should go to the city council meeting tonight, so I did, and . . ."

By the time she's done, I'm tempted to drive right back to Grinberry Falls, hunt down the woman she keeps calling Pink Fingernails, and turn her into No Fingernails.

"How the hell did she find that? I paid an attorney to have it expunged."

"To be fair, you didn't exactly pay the attorney. You blackmailed someone else into paying one for you."

"It was in his best interest. But apparently, his attorney didn't complete the job."

"You never got anything in the mail saying it had been expunged?"

"Probably not if it's still on my record!"

"Glynnie, you never followed up to make sure it had been finalized?"

"I only bothered with it at all because people convinced me I wouldn't be able to get a job after graduation if I didn't. I wasn't asked about it in a single interview. And it hasn't kept me from doing anything since either, so I assumed it was gone. I'd basically forgotten about it."

"Well, it's obviously still findable, so you should probably reach out to that attorney and figure out what happened. Or didn't happen."

"I don't even remember his name."

"Mr. Big probably remembers," Sabrina says.

"We're too old to call him that now." I laugh at the memory of how much *Sex in the City* we watched in college, but my Mr. Big wasn't a tycoon.

"He did have a big dick, though," I say. "Christ, we were nineteen. I can't just look him up out of the blue and say hey, remember that time we got arrested together with our pants down, and your rich daddy hired an attorney to make sure we both spent our junior year on probation instead of going to jail? But then he hired another attorney to get it expunged from your record before graduation, but neither of you bothered to tell me that part?"

She snorts into the wine I know she's drinking because hard conversations call for a glass of wine in her opinion.

"And when you found out, you told his rich daddy if he didn't have his attorney do the same for you, you'd tell his wife you'd been his girlfriend ever since you stopped seeing their son."

"Damn, I had balls of steel for a broke girl with no resources. That man could've had me disappeared. I'm still convinced he might've been in the mob. But I've got a lot more to lose now."

"His son isn't going to have you disappeared for asking for an attorney's name. He'll probably just have his assistant send it to you. I'm sure he and his big dick sit in an executive suite on a top floor somewhere these days."

"This has never once been an issue in my life. I blame you for convincing me to open a Sugar Lips in Grinberry Falls."

"Tell it to somebody who doesn't know what a shrewd business-woman you are."

"Flattery won't excuse your influence."

"I'm just happy to be considered influential. Look up Mr. Big. Ask for the attorney's name and fix this so you never have to deal with it again."

"I will."

My laptop screen is smudged with fingerprints and a sizeable smear of chocolate in the center. I can multitask, but I'm not neat about it. A crumpled coffee shop napkin improves visibility a little. It's good enough.

Mr. Big, aka Landon Bridger is easy to find. And just as Sabrina predicted, he does indeed have an impressive title that I'm sure comes with a big, fancy office. This man is going to think I'm a lunatic.

But then again, I'm pretty sure that's what he thought about me in college, too—and why he liked me so much.

I hit send and exhale. Hopefully, he'll respond.

In the meantime, I may have to do damage control on my reputation in a town where an alpaca is a regular at the local bar and land barons have cows for tenants.

It's time to take my marketing to a more personal level in Grinberry Falls. This may force me to hire someone who can launch a campaign effective enough to drown out negative noise, one that puts me front and center with a wholesome smile on my face.

I'm probably going to have to sponsor a whole youth sports league or a goat pageant or who even knows? Whatever it takes, I'll do it.

Those women don't know who they're dealing with. They can sling all the mud they want. I've outshined better than them. And survived a hell of a lot worse.

I don't want to have to hurt their feelings, but I will. With a wholesome smile on my face.

Rhett's face lights up my screen. I've been expecting this call.

"Hello," I say. "You've reached Angry Blondes with Felonies. How may I help you?"

"What was your crime?"

"I had sex in a car at nineteen."

"That was a felony in Chicago?"

"Apparently, we were within 500 feet of an elementary school."

"During the day while there were kids at the school?"

"Technically, but we were parked in a lot behind an unoccupied building. We didn't even realize that was a school next door. In our defense, it looked more like a church."

"Well, that certainly makes it better."

"There were no kids outside when we got there. And they couldn't see us when they came out because we were literally on the other side of the building from them. We were already done by then, anyway. A cop pulled into the parking lot before we could get all our clothes back on. Who knows what he was planning to do back there if he hadn't found us, but he had apparently had a bad day. He was looking for someone to take it out on, and two half-dressed college kids in a BMW were the perfect targets."

"You couldn't flirt your way out of that?"

"If the entitled asshole I was with had shut up and let me handle it, I'm sure we never would've ended up in handcuffs to begin with."

"Hmm, I'm just going to sit with the image of you half-dressed and in handcuffs for a minute."

"You've seen me fully undressed with my wrists restrained."

"It's an image that never gets old."

"Good to know. Anyway, I thought it had been expunged from my record. I'll get it taken care of so it never comes up again. And I'll spend a bunch of money I don't actually have to spare on a PR firm to make people forget it came up this time."

"Sorry you have to deal with that. I'm also sorry you had to go through what happened back then. Hope the sex was at least worth it."

"We were reckless and stupid with the libidos of nineteen-year-olds, but nothing would've been worth it."

Not even Landon's impressive dick. Owning a Ferrari you don't know how to drive just means you have a nice car, but sadly, nobody's ever going to have a fond memory of the ride. Hopefully, his skills have improved over the years—for his sake and the sake of whomever he's whipping it out for these days. What a waste.

"Saw your general contractor earlier. Looks like your remodel is coming along nicely."

"Oh, damn. If Enzo and his subcontractors find out I have a felony, they're all going to stare at me, trying to figure out what I did."

"For what it's worth, I'm sure they already stare at you."

"Not helpful."

"Listen, I don't like it either, but—"

"Hey, I've got a call coming in from a Chicago area code. I'll call you back."

I click over to the incoming call. "Hello."

"Glynnis Ramsey. I'll be damned. It's been a while."

Of course, he found my number and called instead of just replying to my email like a normal person.

22

Glynnis

S{ABRINA FLIES OUT OF} her front door as soon as she hears my car pull up.

I pull my suitcase from my backseat while she unlocks the cabin. I have my own key, but she apparently wants to hurry things along today.

"I'm glad you're back so soon, but I'm sorry for the reason." She holds the door open for me.

"I can't believe those women are actually protesting with signs and everything. Poor Enzo. He said Pink Fingernails had the nerve to walk inside to inform the plumbers they were working for a felon. She wouldn't leave until he told her he was calling the cops on her for trespassing."

"Thank goodness you've got a new attorney getting that shit erased from your record. It sucks the original guy is retired."

"At least it gave Landon an excuse to send me a dick pic."

"He didn't!"

"Oh, he did. Front and center, which is more than I can say for his hairline these days. Idiot."

"Let me see."

"I deleted it."

"I meant let me see a current picture of his hairline."

"Oh." I pull up his profile.

She takes a quick look and averts her eyes. "Yikes. He needs that big dick now more than ever."

"Yeah, well, I don't. He's recently divorced, too."

"No! Not the recently divorced guy. How many times has he called you since he got your email?"

"I have him blocked if that tells you anything."

"Good."

"I brought twenty signature kits to pass out. It seemed like a lot when I was putting them in my car, but I was in a hurry, and now I feel like I should've brought more."

"You're giving away signature kits? I figured you'd just bring samples to hand out."

"Samples don't change hearts and minds."

"You should put that on a t-shirt."

"Dammit! I meant to grab t-shirts, too."

We park on the other side of Trudy's, not because there are so many protesters—there are just the original three—but because we want to observe how people are reacting to them. Mav told Sabrina people are mostly ignoring them, but I need to see for myself.

Enzo saw my car drive past, so he's come out to talk. I hand him a stack of signature kits.

"Sorry, but we need to set up an outpost in a corner for a little while. We'll be out of your way soon."

"Whatever you need."

Sabrina and I carry the rest of the kits. The trio marching back and forth on the sidewalk recognizes Sabrina. They stop in their tracks and watch us go inside. Maybe they recognize me, too, from internet searches. If not, it shouldn't be hard to puzzle out who I am.

One of the plumbers immediately suggests I have the cops remove the women because they're a liability.

"They have a right to protest," I say. "As long as they keep it outside."

We stack the signature kits in the front corner by the window, and then I pick up three of them and head back outside with Sabrina by my side.

"Good afternoon, ladies. I'm sure you've already connected the dots, but I'm Glynnis Ramsey, the owner of Sugar Lips. I understand you may have some questions for me, but first, I'd like to give each of you one of our signature kits."

I offer a kit to Pink Fingernails. She hesitates, but she takes it. The others seem a little more eager to get their hands on one.

"Inside, you'll find lip scrubs, lipsticks, and lip glosses, all from our signature shades collection. Of course, once we're open, I hope you'll come in and take advantage of our custom color option, too."

Stepping back, I give them space to look at the kits they've been given for a few moments.

"If there is anything you'd like to ask me while I'm here, I'm more than happy to try to clear up any misunderstandings."

Pink Fingernails speaks right up. "I don't understand how you can be licensed to do lip injections if you have a felony conviction."

"To put your fears to rest regarding injections, this location will not offer those services when it opens. They will, hopefully, be added at a later date. And all legal and licensing requirements will be met for any injectionists I hire. I myself, however, am not an injectionist, so my background isn't relevant to that concern."

"How can you hold a liquor license if you have a felony on your record?"

Okay, so her friends are obviously loosening up. This is good. I want to interact with all three of them.

"I won't be applying for a liquor license immediately either. This location will initially open as a storefront only. But if I decide to add the wine and champagne service that is available at our other locations, I'm positive the state of Texas will ensure that I meet all legal requirements to do so."

"Well, that's true," the third protestor agrees. "They won't just hand you a liquor license if you don't meet all the requirements."

Finally, a voice of reason. Maybe it will catch on with the other two.

Silence.

"Is there anything else you'd like to discuss?"

More silence.

"Okay," I say. "I do need to make one thing abundantly clear before I let you get back to your protesting. You are well within your rights to do that out here, but if you set foot inside the building again, I will press charges. Those people are doing their jobs, and you have no right to impede them. It's also a safety liability. Please stay out here until opening day."

I walk back inside. Sabrina follows.

"I don't know how you can stay so calm," she says.

"Inside, I'm seething, but acting calm is the only option I have. Maybe they'll come around. Maybe they'll come back and protest every time I add a new service or when I get a liquor license. But I think Pink Fingernails is the only one who really has a problem with me. The other two seem to be going along to get along."

"Yeah, I think so, too. What are we doing with the rest of these kits?"

"Grab some and come with me to the nail salon."

We hand out kits to the three nail technicians and their clients. They are thrilled and super receptive to hearing more about Sugar Lips. One of the nail techs is the owner, and she wants to talk later about doing a collaborative event.

From there, we walk through Trudy's Diner and give a signature kit to all the staff members who want one. A few of the women say thanks, anyway, but they don't wear lipstick. The dishwasher happily takes one for his girlfriend, though. It's late afternoon, so there are only a few occupied tables, but we have enough kits with us to share one with every woman enjoying an early dinner.

There are still three women protesting me on the sidewalk. But there are four times that many joyfully going through their gifted signature kits in Trudy's.

Merilee shows up as we're about to leave. Sabrina hands her a kit.

"This is for you," she says.

"Really? Oh, wow. This is so nice, Glynnis. Thank you."

"You're so welcome. Do you know my general contractor, Enzo? I recommended he pop in for a meal, and he said he eats here every time he's in town."

"He introduced himself the other day. I've definitely seen him in here before. Nice guy."

"He is nice. So incredibly nice. Kind of hot, too."

Sabrina cuts her eyes at me.

Merilee shrugs. "Yeah, if you like that type."

"What type?"

"I don't know. Cute. Sweet. Salt of the earth, probably super dependable."

"Oh, no. You're not still in your bad boy phase, are you?"

"I'm not sure I was ever in that phase."

"Then, what's your type?"

"Just a little more . . . arrogant, but not an asshole, you know? Confident, maybe to the point of being a little cocky, but a good guy underneath it all. Someone who's as much fun to argue with as anything else, but he won't ruin your life?"

"Wow. I had no idea you and I had that much in common. Does he need to be older, too?"

"Nope. We can be the same age. We just have to be on the same level."

"Got it."

As we walk to the car, Sabrina asks if I'm done trying to play matchmaker for Merilee and Enzo now.

"Oh, come on. You know me better than that."

I set the one remaining signature kit on my backseat. Handing out nineteen in one go wasn't bad, but I definitely wish I'd brought more. I'll have some overnighted.

I'm nowhere near done with my goodwill tour.

23

Rhett

DERRINGER IS BACK IN the studio today. I'm hanging out in the booth even though I'm not needed. It's nice to hear his new stuff, see his progress. When he first entered the scene, people were eager to write him off as another pretty boy singer who wouldn't last.

Those people were wrong. This kid's got what it takes.

Bo goes to the door to let me know he needs out. I squint against the sunlight while he wanders around to find his spot until a squirrel distracts him, and he takes chase. He was a handful as a puppy. Now that he's full-grown, he's calmed considerably, but he still has his hyper moments.

These damn squirrels torment him, and he falls for it every time. He doesn't have a snowball's chance in hell of catching one, but he gives it his all—until the moment he hears her Mercedes drive through the gate.

He abandons the squirrel chase and immediately turns in the direction of her car instead, running next to it when she catches up to him as if he's escorting her onto the property. All animals probably like her, but Bo loves her.

She never shows up unexpectedly, though. I'm not complaining, but I can't help but think something might be wrong.

I climb into my truck and start it up, pulling in front of her to lead the way to the house.

"You okay?" I ask as she steps out of her car and greets Bo with his favorite ear rubs.

"No," she says, walking around Bo and heading for me with an urgency that makes me consider taking a step back.

But then I see the look in her eyes, and I walk toward her instead.

As soon as we meet, she fists my shirt and goes up onto her toes, her lips crushing against mine.

I squeeze her hips to hold her steady and return the angry kiss. It's not me she's mad at, but she's radiating fury. She drops her heels and pushes against my chest without breaking the kiss, taking a small step forward as she continues to shove with the sides of her fists, trying to spur me toward the house.

She wraps her legs around me as soon as I lift her off the ground. I carry her through my front door and kick it closed behind us. Her legs unwind from my waist, and her feet plant on the floor in front of me.

The intensity in her watery stare deepens as she yanks my shirt up to untuck it without bothering to unbuckle my belt. She fills her lungs, and then she rips the snaps open, the popping sound pulling her lids and her shoulders down as she exhales.

Her eyes reopen, and she pushes against my chest again. "I don't want to talk. I just need you to make the whole world disappear right now."

"Take your clothes off."

She follows the order while I unbuckle my belt. Her nipples harden when I pull it through the loops and toss it onto a chair.

"Get on your hands and knees," I say, nodding at the couch.

Her quick compliance is fueled by raw need, and when she's needy and compliant, I am entirely at her service. I'm obeying her requests here as much as she is mine.

My hand rubs over her smooth, soft skin, mapping the curves of her ass. Her lower back tilts up, dipping her spine, and her upper body slides back a few inches, stretching her arms out in front of her and lowering her cheek to the cushion.

I lift her hips to reposition her back onto all fours with her shoulders up. She lets me maneuver her body and holds the pose. I love having her face-down, ass-up, but I need to call the shots right now.

And she needs me to even more.

She draws in a sharp breath at the first stinging slap. My eyes close, and I savor the sounds. Her skin warms quickly under my palm.

When her shoulders begin to sink again, I let her body lower. Her arms stretch over her head, and her cheek rests on the cushion. When she looks up at me, there is no more restless urgency in her eyes, only comfort and compliance.

"Such a good girl, knowing what you need and not being afraid to ask for it."

She bites her bottom lip when the next slap lands, but her face relaxes into a drowsy smile when my hand soothes away the pain. Nothing else is clouding her mind now. As the sting dissipates, so goes her tension.

I could push her a bit further, but I don't think she needs more. She's ready to fully let go.

My middle finger slides into her warm slippery pussy, retracting slowly to massage small circles along her upper wall. Her hips roll slightly to match the motion of my hand like I have her under a spell. I slide another finger inside and begin to thrust them into her, compelling her hips to rock back in the same rhythm.

So needy. So fucking perfect.

I pull my fingers from her tight warmth and use them to trace her lips until her tongue follows, enticing my fingers inside her mouth. She sucks them clean, and my dick lurches at the sensation.

With one hand, I grasp her ankle, pull her leg straight, and flip her over. It doesn't take much effort. Her body assists as if we're sharing the same mind.

Separate minds. Same desires.

"Spread your legs."

Her legs butterfly on my couch, and her body is so serene she looks like she's been painted onto it. But she hasn't fully let go yet.

I crawl between her legs, using my shoulders to nudge them farther apart. My tongue trails through her arousal, tasting and teasing at once. Initially, her only response is a soft moan, but she quickly begins to squirm, bringing her glistening cunt closer to my mouth.

My tongue slides deeper into her, being bathed in her juices and coaxing more to flow. Flattening my tongue, I press it harder against her tender wet pussy until she moans louder for me.

When the tip of my tongue flickers around her swollen clit, her fingers slide into my hair and her back arches. I suck gently, increasing force until it draws up firm under the pressure. Her next moan sounds anguished, but within seconds her breaths deepen, and my favorite words fall softly from her lips.

"Yes, Daddy."

Her orgasm hits hard, sending quakes from her core to her limbs. Having her ride it out on my mouth is the hottest, sexiest fucking thing in the world.

I kiss my way up her spent body, pausing to suck on her nipple, nibbling as it swells, and then drawing it between my lips, lifting my head from her body until it pops free. I repeat the process a few times. Goosebumps race up her arms as the cool air of the room meets her wet nipple, and blood rushes to the stiff peak, blushing it with a deeper shade.

Gorgeous.

Shifting my weight upward, I whisper in her ear. "You're not falling asleep on me, are you?"

"You wouldn't let me fall asleep right now if I wanted to."

"I might. Someday. Stand up."

I stand and help her up, and then I walk her backwards, aiming for the opening of the hallway, but she stumbles, taking us off course. Her back meets the wall between the living room and my bedroom, and this becomes our stopping point because I can't change course again with my dick this hard.

Scrambling to free my erection with one hand, I pin her wrists over her head with the other. She wraps a leg around my waist, pulling my hips forward. I drive into her hard and rough, and she whimpers on my shoulder.

Her post-orgasm-tight pussy spasms before it stretches to take the last few inches as I push up into her with one continuous drive until I'm fully sheathed. She pants a few times when I deliver short, hard strokes until her walls stop seizing on my reentry.

Once she's relaxed enough to easily accept my forceful thrusts, I fuck her like I haven't seen her in weeks, not bothering to make it last.

Her legs shake after I pull my emptied dick out of her.

I've exhausted her, which is exactly what she needed. I carry her to the couch.

"I'll get you a towel, and then you can sleep."

"I don't need to sleep. I just need to be with you. And a towel. And possibly some food."

"Food is a definite possibility."

After she's cleaned up and redressed, we decide on barbecue. Well, I decide, and she says it's fine.

Derringer and his crew are locking up the studio when we drive past. I honk and wave.

"Great," she says. "I'm sure my hair looks like I've just been railed against a wall."

"You always look good with just-been-fucked hair."

"That's not exactly how I want to look in front of a celebrity."

"Your crush on him is cute."

"I do not have a crush on him. He's way too young for me." She flips down her visor and fusses with her hair in the mirror. "Okay. Fine. Me and millions of other women."

"Honesty. Refreshing."

"It doesn't make you jealous?"

"I'm jealous of the wind when it blows over you. But I can handle it."

"Because you know I don't actually want anyone else."

"Because he knows I'd twist his fucking head off if he touched you."

"Don't say things like that. It makes you sound like a Neanderthal."

"You saying you're in the mood for something primal?"

"You're always primal."

"I'm sorry. I'll hold back from now on. Only touch you with gentle caresses. Never say another unrefined word in the heat of the moment."

"You want to make a bet which one of us could handle that the longest?"

I slide my fingers into her hair, gather it in a ponytail, and tug hard enough to tilt her head back slightly. Her hips instinctively rock upward.

"You lose," I say.

"No, you do. That wasn't a gentle caress."

"But you responded positively to it."

"I didn't respond at all."

I slow down for a fox with two kits running across the road.

"You better not be pulling this truck over. I'm not having sex on the side of the road."

"Baby foxes," I say, pointing at the side of the road in question.

She turns just in time to catch a glimpse before they're hidden by the trees.

"Aw, they're so cute! You still lost."

I love that she doesn't even know her hips moved the way they did. Her involuntary reactions are my favorite. She may not consciously feel them, but they rush through me like a power surge. I'm acutely aware of every response in her body.

"Okay, fine. You won."

Both of our competitive energies lie just a scratch below the surface—even for small, meaningless things like this bet that barely existed—and I like to win, but sometimes, she needs it more.

24

Glynnis

SABRINA STANDS BEHIND ME at the cabin's kitchen table. My fingertip scrolls the email that's open on my computer screen one paragraph at a time until she's read the full message from my new attorney.

"This doesn't make sense, Glynnie. If it really was expunged from your record ten years ago, how did that woman find out about it?"

"That's my question. Who is she?"

"I don't know, but we can find out. Go to the city's website. The minutes from city council meetings get posted there."

We pore through the boring minutes until we find her comments. Her name is Shayna Gibson. It takes no time at all to find an online profile. She's an open book, sharing her marital status as "recently divorced – hallelujah!", how many kids she has, the name of the charming small town she's recently moved to . . . and her university alma mater and graduation date.

I did not see that coming.

"She went to college with us, Brina," I say. "Did you know her?"

"No. Are you sure you didn't know her?"

"You and I hung out with all the same people. I guarantee I never met her in Chicago."

"She couldn't have found your arrest online, so she had to have known about it when it happened. Are you positive you didn't know her back then?"

"I have never in my life known anyone named Shayna." I push back from the table. "Oh, shit. I never met her, but Landon's ex before he started dating me was named Shayna."

"There you go. Mr. Big is your connection."

"That asshole just can't stop messing up my life!"

"Well, the good news is you don't have a felony on your record, so clearly your blackmail skills were on point. And you don't have to hire a PR firm. If anyone else tries to find it, nothing will come up. Shayna Gibson will look like an idiot."

"I can't believe I didn't think to search for it myself before I hired an attorney."

"Why would you have thought someone from a decade ago had crawled out of the woodwork to share it from memory? Anyone would've assumed she'd found it online."

"What are the fucking odds?" I say with a sigh.

"Pretty slim. But the fact that you went to college together in Chicago, and ten years later, you both have ties to Grinberry Falls is batshit bonkers."

"You're right. I do need to be grateful that there is no felony to be found."

"Are you sure she was Landon's ex by the time you started going out with him?"

"According to him. She never showed up to make a scene when I was with him, but I know she still called him a lot. I'd forgotten her name until today, but I'm positive that's her."

"I think you need to unblock him and ask him what the deal was between them. Maybe he can reach out to her and get her to stop harassing you."

"He dated her ten years ago. It's not his responsibility to police her behavior now."

However . . . what if two recently divorced people might be into rekindling an old flame? If she's still hot for Landon, and I could be responsible for them getting back in touch, Shayna Gibson would have no reason to try to damage my reputation anymore.

She'd have a reason to be grateful.

There's no reason to think it couldn't work. She's pretty, despite the repressed, unfulfilled drone of misery in her voice. Landon's obviously in the market for a blast from the past. But wouldn't she have already looked him up if she was still interested?

What if she's already reached out and he wasn't responsive?

Maybe I could change his mind. I hold the possibility as an inside thought. Sabrina has reservations every time I get the urge to play matchmaker. It's best to just let her think I'm purely following her advice. Here goes nothing.

I unblock him, but I need some time to think about my next step before I rush ahead. One wrong word, and this guy might end up thinking I'm in the mood to dislocate my jaw for old time's sake.

Muscle memory brings my hand to my cheek. All that soreness for nothing. Thank goodness I wised up in my twenties.

25
Rhett

M AV SHAKES HIS HEAD. "I still can't believe some woman they went to college with lives in Grinberry Falls now."

"You lived in Chicago for a while, and you live here."

"Yeah, but I'm from here."

Derringer and his band walk in, laughing and carrying instruments.

"I didn't know he was playing tonight," I say.

"He called a few hours ago. Nobody else was scheduled, so I told him to come on over."

I pull out my phone.

"Sabrina's probably already told her," Mav says with a grin, proving he knows exactly what I was about to do.

The band sets up while a table of young women stares at them and whispers to each other. I wonder if they're excited because they knew Derringer sometimes plays unannounced shows at Grin's and they can't believe they showed up on the right night, or if they're questioning if that's really him.

Either way, he thrives on attention from fans, so their huddled giggles and gasps are undoubtedly revving up his ego.

The musicians finish setting up and come to the bar to hang out with us while they wait for word to spread.

"I see a local chapter of your fan club is here," I say.

"Not who I was hoping to see in here, though," Derringer responds.

That raises my hackles. If this little shit thinks he's being cute about Glynnis, he might not make it back to that stage.

"Who were you hoping for?" Mav asks. Always one to throw fuel on a fire.

"That waitress from Trudy's. Actually, I'm not sure she's just a waitress. She might be the manager. Every time we're in the same place, I try to get a chance to talk to her, but somehow, it never works out. It's been going on forever, and I'm tired of it. If she shows up tonight, I'm talking to her, even if I have to walk off stage in the middle of a song."

"She's Trudy's daughter," I say. "But you're right. She's not just a waitress. She's also a nurse."

"Damn, the more I learn, the more fantasies she fits."

That shit-eating grin he's known for takes over his face. He's also known for being a notorious player, but it's all media-spun rumors. Derringer wears his heart on his sleeve, and when there's a woman in his life, he walks around looking like a lovesick puppy.

"Hey!" Mav yells, snapping a bar mop at him. "She was my little sister's best friend. Keep her out of your fantasies."

"Yeah, you've made your opinion known before. She's a grown woman. And I can't help where she shows up."

"I'm about to call her to make sure she doesn't show up here tonight."

"Aw, come on, Mav. I just want to get to know her."

I don't say it out loud, but I could see Derringer and Merilee together. Mav doesn't want to hear that any more than I'd want to hear some guy share his fantasies about Twister. Luckily for Derringer, it's Merilee he's hoping to see tonight.

If word of his interest reaches Sabrina, or worse, Twister, they'll bust through the door with their matchmaker hats on. Mav won't stand a chance at keeping Derringer and Merilee apart. Unless she's not interested in him.

Slim chance of that being true.

"Told you Sabrina probably already told her," Mav says, pointing at the front window.

I turn in time to see the two of them walking up to the door. Smiling. It's always good to see her smile.

The bar starts to fill in, and the band takes the stage. It's been a while since she and I have danced together.

I tell myself as I spin her that I need to make more of an effort to date her, not just hang out and have sex. One of us is always coming or going, never together as long as I'd like. But I don't want her to ever feel taken for granted.

Our time together comes easy, and I'm comfortable with her in a way I haven't been with anyone else in a long time. I don't want to get too comfortable, though. She deserves more than that.

I wrap my arm around her, and we walk back to the table we've claimed, along with Sabrina and Joni.

After she sits, I lean over her from behind and kiss her cheek. "You want a drink?"

"Yes, please."

I kiss her again before I walk away. "Love you."

"Love you, too."

Sabrina pretends to gag while Joni acts like she's melting in her chair.

"Can I get the two of you another round as well?"

"After what you just subjected us to?" Sabrina asks. "As quickly as possible."

That was the first time we've said the L-word in front of anyone else, but it felt right. There's no point in hiding it.

26

Glynnis

RHETT AND I GRABBED breakfast tacos on our way to the creek. I have to turn my face into the wind to keep my hair out of my mouth while we eat them, but I don't mind.

Feathery cypress leaves shimmy above our heads, and ripples spread on the water.

"There's always a breeze here," I say. "We don't get much wind in Scottsdale. I miss windy days."

"Wind with no dust storms," he says. "Pretty good selling point."

Why would he say that? Is he trying to sell me on Grinberry Falls? We've agreed to attempt this relationship on a long-distance basis. We haven't talked about either of us relocating. I'm going to assume he's just trying to make me appreciate his hometown a little more since I'll be spending more time here.

I don't respond, just lie back on my forearms and enjoy the breeze on my skin.

He doesn't offer any more selling points.

"Have they started on the electrical work yet?" he asks.

"Tomorrow. Things are moving along. Fingers crossed the project keeps going this smoothly."

"If any problems come up, just remember, there's rarely an issue that can't be fixed. Construction delays are normal. Not the end of the world."

"Why do you expect there to be an issue?"

"It's not an expectation, just reality. It's unusual for there not to be one."

"Well, I pride myself on being an exception in general."

"No argument from me. Wanna go for a ride? It's a nice day for it."

"Where would we be riding to?"

"Just . . . around. All you ever get to see of Grinberry Falls is Mav and Sabrina's, Main Street, and my place."

"And here."

"And the creek." He smiles, and the sky seems bluer behind his dark hair and deep-green shirt.

His beard is freshly trimmed. I prefer it this length, but I don't want to tell him that. I'm not sure why because I usually share my opinions with him freely, but I'd rather quietly admire it.

"Okay," I say. "Let's ride around and see what I've been missing."

There's no denying it's pretty here. So many trees, and I love seeing all the livestock grazing in pastures. No one could be more surprised by that than I am.

Cows. I love seeing cows.

The Texas sun hits different. In Arizona, it cooks your brain like a giant air fryer. Here, it deep fries it, turns your thoughts into battered strips you hardly recognize.

Longhorns! Three of them!

I lean forward and smile at them as though they're sitting in the shade of that oak tree solely for my enjoyment, and I must acknowledge their efforts.

If somebody puts highland cows in one of these fields, I might be sold.

Definitely keeping that thought to myself.

Rhett turns onto a narrow, winding road. Old oak trees stretch across both lanes in either direction, their branches nearly intertwining in a few spots. They form a natural arch. Shards of sunlight tumble through the leaves, stippling the black asphalt ahead with moving fragments in varying degrees of brightness. Like a giant monochrome kaleidoscope being turned.

Oh, wow. This is too enchanting. We need to happen upon some roadkill immediately to break the spell before I open my mouth and let him know just how captivated I am by it all.

"Estate sale!" I shout the words as I read the sign. Some things are beyond my control.

"You want to stop, I take it?"

"Yes, of course. It's an estate sale."

"Right. I don't know what I was thinking."

Why are there so few people here? This giant, Victorian house has to be packed full of treasures. Unless we're too late.

It has all the signs of being day one, though. There are tables in the yard still piled high with dishes and knick-knacks.

A woman in a white blouse with ruffled cap sleeves approaches us. Her brunette bob and chunky, abstract gold earrings announce her authority before she speaks. She's definitely in charge.

"Please feel free to browse the tables. All the furniture inside is also available, and everything in the barn as well. My name is Evelyn. Please let me know if you have any questions."

"Thank you."

I bypass the tables, march up the steps to the porch, and right through the front door. I don't need dishes, but I do need a couch and a chandelier.

"I guess you're looking for furniture," Rhett says.

"We are searching every room in this house, and then we're going through the barn."

"How could we not?"

The front room doesn't have much, just an antique lawyer's bookcase, an old rolltop desk, and a few tattered chairs.

We walk through the kitchen quickly. I glance to the left into the dining room. There is a chandelier, but it's not at all what I'm looking for.

I'm hopeful as we reach the formal living room, but all that remains is a ceiling medallion with a few wires dangling from the hole in the center. Someone beat me to whatever chandelier was hanging in here. I tell myself it was probably ugly, anyway.

Circling back, I head for the stairs.

"There's probably just bedrooms and bathrooms up there," Rhett says.

"I said every room."

"That you did."

He follows me up the stairs, his bootsteps echoing off the wooden treads. As we walk the hallway between the upstairs bedrooms, he manages to find every creaky floorboard.

"How are you able to walk silently in here?" he asks.

"I grew up in a house where stepping lightly was a survival skill."

His hand is warm on my shoulder, massaging gently when he stops behind me as I pause to stare into a bedroom that holds a weird assortment of pieces that don't match at all. They've obviously been consolidated from other rooms.

I almost miss it, but a woman moves out of the way, and there it is.

"That Rococo settee is mine!"

"The coco what?"

I rush across the room and sit on it to stake my claim. My hand fans out next to me, rubbing over the soft burgundy brocade. The carved wood wears an aged patina that highlights the rounded grapes, contrasting with the dark edges of the leaves and vines. It's just worn enough to be unpretentious.

And affordable.

"Can you go let Evelyn know I'm interested in this? I can't leave it for someone else to steal."

"Isn't there a tag you can just peel off and take to her?"

"I'm not paying the price on the tag. She needs to come up here and see me on it. Tell her I have some questions. Do not let her know how badly I want it!"

"Maybe I should guard it while you go find her."

"Oh, hell no. You're not prepared to defend a piece like this from another shopper. Trust me."

"Okay. Try not to hurt anyone while I'm gone."

"Can't hurt anyone who stays at a safe distance."

He attempts a stern look, but he breaks into a smile before he turns away.

Evelyn's a soft touch. I barely even have to negotiate. She has two young men carrying it down the stairs for me within minutes.

If I wasn't with Rhett, I'd have to hire someone to deliver it for me. His truck just became a relationship perk.

Watching the guys load my fabulous find into the bed of the truck, I ask, "Is there any chance I can keep this at your place until I can move it into the store?"

"Yeah, we can stick it in the guestroom where you went through the boxes."

"Is that the most memorable thing I did in that room?"

"Not by a longshot, but we're in public." He steps closer and lowers his voice. "My storage fee might require a few more memorable acts."

"Just let me know what I owe, Daddy."

"I'll let you know all right."

The guys hop down and slam the tailgate, interrupting our discussion of Rhett's storage terms.

I open my purse, but Rhett pulls his wallet out and tips them before I can reach mine.

"Is there much in the barn?" I ask them before they walk away.

They both nod.

"Yeah," one of them says. "It's mostly a bunch of boxes, but there are some old light fixtures."

"Old light fixtures, huh? Color me intrigued."

Rhett sighs. "This thing isn't enough? You're going to make me dig through a bunch of boxes now, aren't you?"

"I'll regret it if I don't at least take a peek."

There are no other vehicles parked by the barn. I love that we might be the only ones out here. I can take my time with no one else breathing down my neck, trying to beat me to something great.

Rhett pulls the giant splintered doors open, and dust motes twirl through the air to greet us. It's almost magical, such graceful allergens. As soon as I think the word, I sneeze.

And then I sneeze again. And again.

"You sure you want to dig around in here?"

"That's why women invented allergy meds."

"Women invented all of the allergy meds?" he asks.

"Probably."

"Well, as long as your research is sound."

"I don't need to do research to know that men throughout history have taken credit for women's work." *Achoo! Achoo! Achoo!* "Damn allergy sneezes. They always come in threes."

"I'll get you some allergy meds on the way home."

"You should know that antihistamines knock me out."

"Now you tell me."

I suck in a long breath.

"Are you okay?"

He's at my side before I can speak.

"That was a breath of amazement, not an asthma attack."

His eyes roam around the dusty barn. "What exactly are you amazed by?"

"That!" I point at a naked chandelier. Three tiers. French Empire. Be still my heart. "Please let all the crystals be here."

I kneel next to it to examine the brass. A few minor scratches, but nothing is broken. I pull on the box next to it and realize it's heavy—heavy enough to be full of cut-glass droplets and beads.

"Can you cut this tape?"

He pulls out a pocketknife and slices through the yellowed packing tape.

Laying my hands over the box flaps, I send up a quick prayer before I lift them to look inside.

Smaller boxes. So many of them. My pulse hastens. "I think they're here!"

"I'll go get Evelyn."

"No! Not yet. We have to count them to be sure none are missing. And then we have to inspect them all for cracks or chips."

He peers into the box. "Do you know how many of those boxes are in there?"

"Hopefully, the perfect number." *Achoo! Achoo! Achoo!*

I sit cross-legged and start to line the little boxes up around me.

Rhett throws his head back and groans. And then he sits next to me with his knees bent and helps me organize the boxes into rows by size.

"Count the spaces for crystals on the bottom tier."

He counts while I open boxes and carefully unwrap crystals. When he gives me the final count, we set aside that number.

We repeat the process until we've counted and inspected a crystal for every slot and the strands that drape between the tiers. Like the brass, there are a few scratches, and there are some tiny chips here and there, but nothing that will even be noticeable once it's hung.

"I cannot wait to polish this brass and clean all this glass until it sparkles."

Achoo! Achoo! Achoo!

"Please wait outside in the fresh air while I go find Evelyn," he says.

I refuse to leave the chandelier and crystals unattended. He'll eventually get the drill. He helps me repack the little boxes into the larger one, and then he carries it outside. I bring the brass frame, only stopping to sneeze twice.

Evelyn seems surprised when she realizes the box holds all the crystals. It was in plain sight. Whoever catalogued the inventory for this sale, must not have realized the light fixture was a chandelier.

A real-deal vintage, French Empire three-tiered chandelier in good condition!

I sneeze in triplicate again, and she jumps back as if I might infect her with the plague.

"Make me an offer," she says.

I have to make her three offers (and sneeze three more times) before we agree on a price.

Rhett puts the chandelier in the backseat of his truck. I'm impressed that he didn't try to put it in the bed, but I clearly underestimated him. I don't do that often anymore.

He makes sure of it.

27

Rhett

I CALL IN A favor with one of the ranch hands, asking for some help to move this couch thing into my house. It's heavier than it looks. We set it in the middle of the bedroom, and I tell him it's fine there so he can get back to work.

But when Twister dozes off on my normal couch, I push this thing enough to clear it from the center of the room. When I bend down to straighten the corner of the rug that got caught under one of the legs, I spot something under the bed.

Lying on my side, I stretch my arm to pull it out. As soon as my hand wraps around it, I know what it is. How it got there, I have no idea. It must be from one of the boxes she went through, but I never saw it, and I know she didn't either.

She would've said something about this.

I guess it could've fallen out of one of them when I first brought the boxes home. There were other things I stored in here until family members could come over and go through it all, too. I'll probably never know how it ended up there.

But I know it's time to hire a housekeeper. Nothing should've gone undetected under that bed for this long.

"Hey, I've gotta go!" she calls from the couch.

"Go where?" I walk down the hall to find her putting her shoes on.

"Just got a message from Enzo. The building inspector issued a stop work order!"

"Did he say why?"

"No. He said to call him so he could explain. I knew this was all going too smoothly." She stands and looks me in the eye. "You didn't have anything to do with this, did you?"

"I have no control over building inspectors. But even if I did, I wouldn't have done anything to sabotage you. Do you really think I would do that?"

"You didn't want me to buy the place. You've told me repeatedly that Main Street isn't a good location for me."

"Yeah, I did say that a few times, but not since construction started. Whether I think it's the right location or not, I wouldn't do anything to hurt you or your business. Call Enzo and see what he has to say."

"I'm just driving over there. I'd rather discuss it in person."

"He might not even be there. If a stop work order was issued, they literally have to stop until the problem is resolved."

"I don't even know what the problem is!"

"That's why you need to call Enzo!"

"Stop yelling at me!"

I lean against the wall and take a deep breath, exhaling slowly. "I'll drive."

"Fine, but I do not need you to get in the middle of it when we get there. It's my business, and I can handle it."

Why does she insist on testing me like this? If she would just call the man . . .

"Well, let's go," she says. "We need to get there before everybody leaves."

I grab her purse that she left on the coffee table because I know for a fact that her keys are in it and follow her out the door.

Enzo is sitting out front in his truck when we pull up. He looks like he'd rather wrestle a bear that have the conversation that's coming.

I don't see any of the trucks that were parked out here when the plumbers were working inside. No truck with an electrician's name or logo either. Work has definitely shut down.

Frankly, I'd also rather fight a bear than hear this conversation.

We all step out at the same time. Three truck doors close in unison, hers with more of a slam than I think is necessary.

"What happened?" she asks as we all walk toward each other.

Enzo puts one hand up defensively—never a good sign.

"There is a problem with the electrician's permit."

"I thought the permits were all obtained weeks ago!"

"There was a change to the plans once the plumbing got under-way. All the permits were updated except electrical."

"Why didn't you update that one?"

"I pull the primary building permit. Subs are responsible for their own, and they have to be amended if changes are made. The plumbing changes affect the electrical, but the electrician didn't get his filed in time. It's been filed now. I've talked to the building inspector, but there's no way around it."

"Shouldn't you have been on top of this?" she asks.

"Yeah, I should have. He said he'd filed it, and I assumed his update had gone through like everyone else's. Turns out, he doesn't file his own permits. Someone in his office handles them."

"And mine got mishandled. Lucky me."

"I work with this guy a lot. He's never not had his permits in order. When the building inspector showed up this morning, I was on another jobsite, so it took a little while for me to sort out what had happened. I'm not going to make excuses for either of us, Glynnis. He didn't follow up with his staff about the permit, and I didn't follow up with him."

"So, you both just assumed it was handled?"

"That's pretty much the gist of it. Like I said, I'm not going to make excuses. I'm incredibly sorry it's happened, but the good news is the amendment should be cleared much quicker than the original permit."

"If it's cleared! What happens if it's not?"

"It'll be refiled until it is. But there's no reason it shouldn't be approved. For what it's worth, the building inspector agrees. This is just a formality."

"It may be nothing more than a formality for you, but I'm trying to nail down an opening date, and if I can't trust that you're going to be on top of your contractors, I can't do that. I'm the one who gets stuck in limbo. I'm the one whose business gets put on hold. I'm the one whose loan may have to be extended, which means I'm the one who'll be paying more interest! Unforeseen delays are one thing, Enzo, but this was preventable."

"It was. But we didn't prevent it, so now we have to deal with it. If you have to extend your financing, I'll cover any additional charges you owe. It's my mistake, and I'll pay for it."

"How much more time?"

"Building inspector said probably a couple of weeks."

"How many other jobs are you currently overseeing?"

"With all due respect, Glynnis, I don't owe you that information. But I do owe it to you to ensure that nothing else slips through the cracks on your job. You have my word on that."

She stares at him like she's not sure if she wants to punch him or thank him. I'm pretty sure she's going to do the right thing here, but I hope his reflexes are sharp, just in case.

I clearly see the problems this causes for her, and I agree it shouldn't have happened, but I feel for the guy because you can't look left or right around here without seeing some type of construction going on. And when you're self-employed, you've got to take the work while it's plentiful. It's highly possible he may have taken on a little more than he should have, but mistakes happen, regardless.

He's owning up to it, not trying to bullshit her in any way. As far as stop work orders go, this one seems like an easy fix. It's an administrative oversight, not the result of faulty work that has to be redone.

She's not going to want to hear any of that, at least not right away.

Enzo extends his hand, and I internally flinch.

It takes her a few beats, but she shakes his hand. "I can't afford any more delays."

"Neither can I," he says.

He's being calm and professional with her, but I bet that electrician left with his balls hiding in his ribcage. Enzo's eyes are clouded with partially diffused anger, vapors of a recent eruption that hasn't fully settled yet.

I hope he goes straight home after this because he's showing all the signs of somebody who could blow all over again if the slightest thing provokes him. Can't say that I blame him, but it's done.

"Let's all go next door and grab a bite to eat," I say. "There's nothing more that can be done here, and everything looks better after a slice of Trudy's pie."

Twister turns her ambiguous gaze on me. I know she's going to tell me later that I shouldn't have gotten involved, but she doesn't look mad . . . not entirely. What's going on behind those eyes?

"Yeah, let's eat," she says.

Enzo attempts to politely decline our invitation, but she's not having it.

"I said let's eat. That meant you, too."

I clear my throat to break the tension. My own, to be clear. "Even on the bad days, you've still gotta eat."

"All right," he says. "But I'm buying."

Merilee comes over to wait on us, and Glynnis goes from somber to effusively friendly in an instant. I know she likes Merilee, but this sudden mood change is over the top.

"I recognize that lipstick shade. It looks great on you."

"Thanks. I've gotten quite a few compliments on it. I think half the hospital staff will be instant Sugar Lips customers."

"I appreciate that more than you know." She turns to Enzo. "Did you know Merilee was also a nurse?"

He looks lost. How the hell would he have known that?

"I did not. That's an honorable job."

Merilee smiles. "It's a shitty job at the moment, but I do enjoy being a nurse in general."

"Did you know Enzo owns his own company?" Twister asks. "I think that's impressive at his age."

Ohhhh, now I understand. I thought matchmaking was supposed to be subtle. She couldn't be any more obvious.

"It is indeed impressive," Merilee says. "Congratulations." She and Enzo exchange a knowing look.

How could they not know? But that look also has a very polite, friends-only vibe. There is zero spark between them.

"You should take a break and join us," Glynnis says as if Trudy's isn't full of customers.

"Or I could take your order."

"What time do you get off? Maybe we could all walk over to Grin's after we eat."

Enzo cuts in. "Don't include me in that plan. I have a mountain of paperwork I need to get home and take care of."

"Paperwork, huh?" Glynnis narrows her eyes at him. "Well, we'd hate to be the reason any of that fell through the cracks."

"Maybe next time," I say, prompting her to narrow her at eyes at me instead.

Our dinner conversation devolves into poor Enzo being pumped for personal information like she's writing his biography.

He's so ready to get out of the hot seat that he declines a slice of Trudy's pie.

After we part ways on the sidewalk, she and I cross the street to go to Grin's alone.

"You realize they're not at all into each other, right?" I ask.

"I know. But they don't really know each other either."

"Typically, people only want to get to know each other if there's an initial spark."

"That's not true. Some people go all the way from enemies to lovers."

"I'm not saying the spark can't start out negative and turn positive, but those two are completely neutral. There is zero charge in the air between them. None."

"Fine. But they both need to be set up with someone. They're too young to be lonely."

"You have no idea if they're lonely."

"Trust me. I have a heightened sense when it comes to recognizing loneliness."

"As long as I'm around, you never have to worry about being lonely."

She reaches for my hand. I feel a quick twinge in my chest, remembering how she asked me if I was responsible for the stop work order. Probably just heartburn. I shouldn't have eaten all of my pie and then finished off the second half of hers.

But I hate that she believed I might've tried to harm her in any way.

I hold the door open for her and tell myself she might not even see the three women sitting at a table in the center of the bar—staring right at us.

It's either my lucky night or she sees them and intentionally ignores them.

Joni and Sabrina are toasting at the bar.

"What's the occasion?" I ask.

"A new film being partially shot in Grinberry Falls," Sabrina says.

"And a payday for me that'll cover Oliver's feed and medications for the next year," Joni adds.

I mind my own business when it comes to other people's finances, but I know Joni's not hurting for money. She's cautious by nature. Sometimes, I wish she'd go a little crazy, splurge on herself. God knows she deserves it. Her husband died young, and I know he had insurance, and she was able to pay off the house, but she spends too much time in it if you ask me. She works part-time in a veterinary clinic, and I'm not sure she really even needs to do that. I think she does it to stay busy.

"Would your boss mind if I came by the vet clinic to hand out signature kits to the staff?" Twister asks.

"No, not at all. She's big on self-care. She's always giving one of us a gift certificate for a massage or to get our nails done."

"Oh, I need the info for that massage therapist if they're any good."

"I'll send it to you. Pop in the clinic whenever you want. You'll find a very appreciative group of women."

"Great. I've got a new shipment coming tomorrow."

Pink Fingernails approaches us. Here we go . . .

"I notice work has stopped on your renovation," she says.

"How very observant of you. Nothing more than a slight delay. Sugar Lips is still coming."

"What happened?"

"Don't pat yourself on the back. It wasn't a result of your efforts." Twister focuses like a tiger about to pounce. "Were you this much of an activist when we were going to college together?"

"Y-you remember me?"

"No. But you obviously remembered me. Why is that?"

"We had more in common back then than you'd probably ever guess."

"Was it Landon's enormous dick? Is that what we had in common?"

Enormous. There's a word you don't hear every day. Unless maybe if you're Landon, whoever the fuck he is.

Pink Fingernails blinks repeatedly like a relay in her brain just short-circuited.

"If it helps at all," Twister says, "As far as I knew, you were his ex. Was that not true?"

"We probably would've gotten back together if you hadn't come along. All you wore were tight jeans and low-cut sweaters. You were obviously willing to do anything for attention."

"Slut-shaming at your age? Really? I wore what I felt comfortable in, and I did what I wanted with who I wanted, but I was a girl's girl. Single guys weren't that hard to find."

"Not for you, I'm sure."

"I'm trying really hard to give you the opportunity to behave like a grown-ass woman here. But speaking of single guys, Landon is recently divorced. Did you know that?"

"No. He hasn't said anything on his socials."

"Ah, you stalk his socials."

"I don't stalk them. We happen to follow each other. We have for years."

"Not everyone uses social media like group therapy. Some people still manage to keep their private life private."

"How do you know he's divorced?"

"We talked recently."

Oh, good. They're still in contact.

"Of course you did," Pink Fingernails says, accusingly.

"Are you blind? Can you see this man sitting next to me? What on earth would make you think I could possibly be interested in Landon Bridger when I'm fucking this guy?"

Okay, I don't hate that.

Pink Fingernails reverts to blinking mode for a moment.

"So, Landon's aged a little. He's incredibly successful."

"You should send him a message. Trust me, the likelihood of him responding is incredibly high."

"And say what? Remember that girl who came between us in college and let you fuck her in a car in broad daylight and you got arrested together and it was all your friends could talk about and it broke my heart into a million pieces and I ended up marrying a narcissist piece of shit because of it? Well, guess what? She sells lipstick now, and she's opening a store in the town where I live. Small world, huh?"

"He's aware you and I have seen each other. But I am in no way responsible for who you chose to marry. Or for your broken heart. I didn't even know you."

"You wouldn't have bothered to know me back then."

"It doesn't sound much like you wanted to know me back then either," Twister says. "You also don't know me now. How does what you're trying to do to me now rectify anything that happened in the past?"

"Are you sure he's divorced?"

"All signs point to yes. And pretty sure he hasn't dated much since it became final."

"Do you think he's ready to date?"

"Oh, he's ready and willing."

"Have you gone out with him since his divorce?"

"Noooooo. Listen, as memorable as his dick may be, I wouldn't get on a plane to see it again. But then again, I was never in love with the guy. If you were, shoot your shot. What've you got to lose?"

I just can't get enough of hearing about this guy's memorable dick.

"Just what's left of my self-esteem."

"You're beautiful. Your self-esteem should be through the fucking roof. I'm sorry anyone ever made you feel like you were less than. I personally think you could do a lot better than Landon, but that's none of my business."

"You told him what I was doing to you, didn't you?"

"It may have come up."

"Great. He probably thinks I'm a bitter divorcée with an ax to grind."

"I could reach out to him to let him know it was all just a big misunderstanding. I mean, if that's what it was."

Oh, good. By all means, please reach out to him.

"I guess maybe it was. I'd actually really appreciate it if you'd lay some positive groundwork before I contacted him."

"Okay. Annnnnd?" Twister drags out the word, waiting for her expected quid pro quo to be defined.

"And I'll stay away from Sugar Lips. I just need to say one last thing. That is such a stupid name for a business."

"That stupid name grossed eight figures last year."

"Damn. Respect. Low eight at least?"

"Just imagine whatever number makes you feel better."

"Got it. I really like the lip gloss, by the way."

"Spanked by Cupid looks good on you."

"You knew I was wearing your product this whole time?"

"From the moment you walked up. I guess you disapprove of the name of the shade, too?"

"I don't love it."

"Come by the store when you run out. Your money spends the same, whether you're proud to be there or not."

"I'll wait a few days before I reach out to Landon."

"I'll send you a message after I talk to him," Twister says.

"But you don't know . . . oh, you've already seen my socials."

"Had to do a little homework to figure out who you were."

"Right. Enjoy the rest of your night."

She goes back to her friends, and Twister sips her martini like nothing happened.

"Enormous, huh?" I ask.

I tried to leave it alone, but that particular adjective makes jealousy a lot harder to contain.

"I mean . . ." She brings her hands up, clearly about to use them to illustrate a measurement.

I clasp my hands over hers and lower them to the bar top. "No."

Her giggle is not as cute as she thinks it is. But she did say she prefers my dick over his. That's what I heard, anyway.

She blows me a kiss, and I smile like a fucking sap—a jealous one, but not as much as I was a few minutes ago. She knows exactly how to charm me into focusing on all the right feelings.

Not all witches wear pointy hats.

28
Glynnis

R HETT LIFTS MY CARRY-ON to put it in the overhead bin. I was surprised when he offered to spend more time in Scottsdale with me so soon.

He's familiar enough with my city now that he has favorite restaurants and knows all the alternate routes to avoid the freeway. He prefers to get outside of town, though, says it because he hates all the traffic.

But I think it's because he's captivated by the desert, especially at night. It's hypnotic. You'd have to be emotionally numb not to feel it

I suggest my favorite wine bar for sunset drinks and tapas, and he doesn't balk at making the forty-five-minute drive. As we drive in, he smiles at all the scurrying chipmunks just as much as I do.

And when we leave after the sun has gone down, following a scenic, winding road, I see the awestruck expression on his face at the way the rising full moon and all the stars make the perfect backdrop for a giant saguaro standing alone.

It's beautiful here; it's just a different kind of beautiful, other-worldly compared to what he's used to. But you can love two places at once.

Not that I'm necessarily in love with Grinberry Falls, but I don't feel as dismissive about it as I did before I spent so much time there. It's grown on me, but I still need this.

When we get back to my condo, he asks if I have a ladder.

"Why?"

"Because that lightbulb needs to be replaced." He points up to a recessed light in my kitchen.

"You don't have to do that."

"Who normally does it?"

"Me."

"So, the answer is yes, you have a ladder."

"I can change a lightbulb. These ceilings aren't even that high."

"I'm quite sure you can. Where's the ladder?"

"In the garage, and I have a claw thingie that extends to grab the bulb."

"I don't need the claw thingie."

He goes to the garage and comes back carrying my ladder with one hand. "Is this it? A stepladder?"

"Yeah, but when you use the claw thingie—"

He pinches the bridge of his nose. "And where would I find that?"

"It's in the closet under the stairs. I'll get it."

He changes the bulb, returns the claw thingie to me, and takes my ladder out to the garage. When he comes back into my now well-lit kitchen, he announces he's buying me a real ladder before he leaves town.

I've never needed a bigger ladder, but if it makes him feel better to know there's one that meets his standards stored in my garage, so be it, I guess.

"Thanks for changing the bulb."

"You're welcome."

I yawn, and he turns out the lights.

When I pull back the comforter on my bed, he laughs.

"What is that, a fur sheet?"

"It's a waterproof blanket."

"Oh," he says, his eyebrows drawing together as if this is the first he's hearing of such a thing.

"We had a whole conversation about buying one of these."

His sudden grin signifies it's coming back to him now. "Why do you still have clothes on?"

"**A**RE YOU SURE YOU can't fly back home with me?" Rhett asks, sitting on my couch with his boots in his hand. "I'm not tired of your face yet."

"I am home. And it's not my face that you're not tired of."

I walk close enough for him to wrap an arm around my waist.

"I'm not tired of any of you, including your face. A few days wasn't long enough."

"Stay longer."

"I would if I could." He drops his arm and puts on his boots.

"As soon as that updated permit is issued, I promise I'll be back in Grinberry Falls long enough for you to get sick of all of me."

"How long do you plan on staying?"

"Probably until we've been open at least a month."

"Really?"

"Yeah. After electrical is done, we've still got drywall, flooring, and painting, and I want to be around to keep tabs on those stages. Plus, I want to be there the moment I'm able to get in to start stocking and decorating. And I'll have to be sure my staff is fully trained before I leave them on their own. The staff I haven't hired yet."

He stands and brushes away the annoying section of hair that won't stay out of my eyes this morning. "I won't get sick of having you around. If I thought I could bribe somebody to speed up that permit, I'd do it."

"You could always try."

His phone buzzes, and I know what it means before he looks at it.

"My ride's here."

He wouldn't let me drive him to the airport, so this is it.

Our goodbye kiss stirs a sadness I've been desperately trying to ignore ever since we got out of bed. I miss him already, and he's still standing right in front of me.

But leaving each other is part of our deal. There's no way around it.

After he's gone, I strip the bed so I can start laundry, picking up the waterproof sheet we discarded after we broke it in last night on my way out of the bedroom. I'll definitely be buying one of these for his place. Maybe I should get one for Mav and Sabrina's cottage, too.

Flash flooding is imminent anywhere he and I share a bed.

Come on with that damn permit, already!

29

Glynnis

I ARRIVE IN GRINBERRY Falls a little ahead of the app's predicted time, feeling victorious to have beaten it once again, but I don't actually have anywhere to be.

Sabrina is out of town for work, so there's no need to rush over to the cottage. As anxious as I am to see Rhett, he's got a committee meeting this evening, so he's unavailable for at least an hour.

I'm curious about the new shopping center I always pass on my way into town. If I'm going to be here for weeks on end, I may as well see what's available out here on the concrete edge where old-timers won't dare to tread.

Driving through the parking lot, I wait for a store to appeal to me. There are some good ones, but none that call my name after a twelve-hour drive. But the moment I spy the non-chain coffee shop

I can already smell the roasted beans and feel the caffeine perking me up.

Oh, this place is nice. Very loungey. Wood floors, modern chandeliers with amber bulbs to keep the lighting plentiful, but soothing. No hard chairs. They cater to campers—those of us who show up with our laptops and our long digital to-do lists. My kind of place.

I can see myself working from one of these high-back clamshell chairs, my own little privacy pod. In fact, I'm about to test one out right now.

A pair of high-school girls vacates two of them, and I take the one facing away from the window. I'm tired and prone to distractions. If I can see the sidewalk, I'll people watch instead of checking tasks off my list.

There are a couple of low tables surrounded by six oversized club chairs right behind me, but they're all empty, so I don't bother with headphones. It's nice and quiet in here, aside from the sound of clicking keyboards and the soft music playing.

I honestly couldn't ask for a better vibe.

I'm lost in an array of online wallpaper samples when something splinters my attention. It takes me a second to switch gears from my all-consuming visual comparisons to listening . . . it's a male voice, followed by another.

Great. Sounds like a group of men is settling into the large chairs behind me, and they obviously came for conversation.

I search my laptop bag for my earbuds, but then a familiar voice chimes in.

What's Rhett doing here? The committee must've decided on a change of venue for their meeting. Interesting.

Don't mind me. I'm just a fly on the wall—a super intrigued fly, who'd love to hear what exactly this little private committee is currently plotting.

"Well, even with my shirt still wet, I have to admit, this place is a lot more comfortable than city hall."

Why is his shirt wet?

One of the other men says, "I don't know what made those damn fire sprinklers malfunction like that."

Oh, damn, that's funny. Wish I could've seen it happen.

"Hell, who knows." Rhett's voice is laced with only the slightest hint of agitation.

I smile, telling myself he's more easygoing than usual tonight because he knows he'll be seeing me as soon as his meeting is over.

Sooner than he thinks.

The men exchange small talk, nothing official sounding. I wonder if they even have any business to cover, or if they're just meeting because it was on their schedule.

Then one of them gets a little personal.

"So, you still seeing that Blonde who's opening the lipstick store?"

"Yeah, I'm still seeing her, Eldon."

"Well, she got one over on us, but it won't happen again. Our CC&Rs are all in line with our mission now."

They all mutter some form of agreement. I guess their attorney found a legal way to shut out any other non-locals who want to set up shop on Main. Well, good for them, but he's right about me outsmarting them.

I grin over the rim of my coffee cup.

"She calls it a lip *spa*, doesn't she?" one of the other voices asks.

"Yeah, that's what it's called," Rhett says. "They're pretty popular from what I can tell."

"Sounds like some kind of passing beauty fad to me. I hope she's got a back-up plan for when the next new trend comes along. Mortgage companies won't take lipstick as payment."

They all laugh. All of them.

Then one of them says, "I hope she hasn't bitten off more than she can chew. Once some women get mad, they let their emotions lead, and they'll do just about anything to prove a point, even if it leads straight to bankruptcy."

"She's definitely hardheaded."

That's his response to a man basically calling me financially stupid?

"Well, at least she's pretty."

More laughter. Rhett better have a better response to that comment than the last one. And quick.

"I get what you're saying, trust me," he says. "I can't imagine anybody making a living selling lipstick for the long-term either. Her other locations offer lip injections, too, and—"

"Oh, good lord. I hope she doesn't bring that service to Grinberry Falls. We don't need every woman in town walking around with fish lips."

Fish lips? I'll fish-lip you, motherfucker! No woman has ever walked out of a Sugar Lips looking like a damn fish!

"I think it's definitely in her plans for the future, but—"

"How much of a future can a business called Sugar Lips have? Nan says she's put in a permit for a neon sign. Never thought I'd see the day there'd be pink neon lips on Main Street."

"I couldn't have predicted it myself."

That's it? That's all he's got to say? He couldn't have predicted my sign?

"Like I said, I understand your concerns," he goes on, again agreeing with this opinionated old jackass who knows fuck-all about me or my business.

I slam my cup on the side table to my right, shove my computer back into its bag and hook it onto my shoulder along with my purse before I bust out of my clamshell of privacy to confront him.

I'm not even in front of him yet when he opens his mouth again. "It's definitely not a name I would've chosen, but—"

"Is that right, Rhett? You wouldn't have chosen it?"

The color drains from his face when he sees me, hears me, and hopefully, feels my fury slice right through his cowardly core all at once.

"Newsflash! I don't give a flying fuck what you would've chosen. Because it's not your business! It's mine! I created the product that launched it, and I'm damn proud of it. What have you ever created?"

My angry gaze scrapes over his cohorts. "What has any of you ever created, other than wrong assumptions and a small-minded fear of the world outside Grinberry Falls? Well, guess what? This little town's growing, whether you like it or not. Soon, it's going to outgrow your small minds, and I know that scares the absolute shit out of every one of you."

I take a step back so I can properly look down at them. "Die scared. I'll be busy selling lipstick on Main Street under the brightest pair of flashing pink neon lips south of the goddamn Vegas strip to your grandchildren's grandchildren! And if they want lip injections, you can bet your ass I'm going to make sure they get the most state-of-the-art service available!"

Rhett leaps to his feet when I take a step forward. "Twister, wait."

Wait, my ass. I waited for you to speak. That was my last mistake of the night.

"Glynnis!"

Nope.

I power-walk all the way to my car, listening for his boots on the sidewalk behind me.

He never leaves the coffee shop.

30

Rhett

I'VE NEVER PLEADED SO hard from a barstool in my life. Or from anywhere else, but if I can just talk to her.

"Sabrina, can you at least tell me where she is? It's been over a week. She won't respond to my messages. Won't answer my calls. She's not at your place. She's not at her store. Did she go back to Scottsdale? I'll get on a plane. Just tell me if she's there."

"I can tell you that she's safe, and she doesn't want to see you right now."

"But if I can just talk to her."

"She's not ready to hear your voice, Rhett. The last words she heard you say are still pretty fresh."

"It's the words she didn't hear me say that are the problem."

"I agree."

"Then help me talk to her."

"Do you know how deep her trust issues run? Do you have an ounce of a clue how much it took for her to drop her defenses and trust you?"

"I know. But you know I wouldn't have intentionally done anything to hurt her."

"My loyalty is to her."

"So is mine! But I can't straighten this out if I can't even talk to her."

"Give it time is all I can tell you."

I silently nod and leave the bar. It's not until I look in my rearview mirror that I realize the nod is still happening. I'm so numb I can't even feel my own body in motion.

It's raining when I get to the creek, but it doesn't matter. I wasn't planning to get out of the truck anyway. Just need to sit here for a while.

When I get home, Bo rushes from the shelter of the porch to meet my truck. How'd he get outside? I left him in the house . . . it replays in my head, the way I stormed out the door, never doublechecking to make sure he was in. If he'd followed me out, I wouldn't have known.

This has got to stop. I can't keep walking around with my mind somewhere else. Sabrina's right. There's nothing I can do but give it time.

I stand under a blazing hot shower, hoping it will help clear my head. As if sinus congestion is my problem. It can't hurt.

When the rain finally stops, I drive to Trudy's for dinner. There's nothing to eat in my house. No point in buying groceries because I have no interest in cooking. I want what's easy.

I need something to be easy.

If she would've just waited, just listened. If I'd known she was going to go into hiding, I'd have gone after her. I thought I was giving her space.

Merilee gives me sad puppy eyes as soon as I walk in. I guess the whole town knows. Joni looks up from her menu and offers the weakest smile I've ever seen on her face. That woman doesn't do pity, but I'll be damned if I can think of another way to describe it.

I consider getting my food to go, but I don't want to go home and eat alone either.

The chair legs scrape against the floor. Joni's smile widens. "You never were one to wait for an invitation."

"Your smile was so inviting I couldn't help myself."

"She'll come around, Rhett."

"Have you met Glynnis?"

"Saw her a few hours ago in fact. She came by the clinic. Brought some products for the staff."

"She's still in town?"

"You didn't hear that from me."

"How was she?"

"All business. Very much in marketing mode. Big, empty smile on her face. You're going to have to give her some time."

"You're the second woman today who's given me that advice, and I didn't like hearing it the first time either. Where's she staying?"

"She needs time, Rhett."

"Do you really think it's fair for her to have to keep walking around hurt and confused when I could fix it if you'd just tell me where she is?"

"Oh, don't you dare try that manipulative shit with me. You knew that wasn't going to work before the words ever left your mouth."

"I'm not trying to manipulate you."

"Maybe not consciously, but you're hurting and you're reaching for any tactic that might work. Pull your head out of your ass and don't try that on anybody else."

"Have you ever thought of becoming a therapist?"

"No."

"Good. You'd be terrible at it."

She laughs, and we find other topics to talk about while we eat. I'm sure this chicken parmesan is good because I've eaten it more times than I could count, but I can't taste it tonight.

"How's your chicken parm?" I ask.

"Probably the same as yours."

"Oh, right. We ordered the same thing."

"Keep eating it. You brain clearly needs more fuel."

THE PILLOWCASE UNDER MY cheek still smells like her. I toss and turn a few more times, knowing it's not going to make a damn bit of difference.

My eyes open wide. I wonder if she's staying in Joni's garage apartment. That would make sense. She could park behind it, and I'd never see her car.

Not that I can go over there and snoop around without Joni filling my ass with buckshot.

I like thinking that's where she's at. Feels safer than a motel, and that's all there is around here. The closest decent hotel is an hour away.

When I close my eyes again, I imagine her sleeping soundly in Joni's apartment. It helps a little to convince myself she's not that far away. Safe and sound. Close by.

We'll talk soon. She just needs time.

31
Glynnis

THE FLOORS WERE FINISHED two days ago. They look great. Drywall coating is cured. Tomorrow morning, the painters come. Inventory will start arriving by the end of the week. The counter and cabinets get installed next week. And then I can bring in all the pretty things for the final transformation that will make it officially a Sugar Lips lip spa.

Interviews start in two days. I wasn't sure how much interest my job postings would get, but it turns out there are a lot of women in the area looking for part-time work. I've got a couple of good candidates for a manager, too.

It's starting to feel real. When I look around the space now, it's hard to remember what it looked like before.

I jump when someone knocks on the back door.

"Why would you do that without sending me a message to let me know you were coming? I thought it was going to be him."

Sabrina stares at me. "What if it had been?"

"Can we not go there, please?"

"Okay." She steps inside and closes the door behind her. "But it's been a while, and you're going to be in town for a while longer. You're going to run into him eventually."

"Not if I can help it."

"That's what I'm saying, though. You're not going to be able to help it, Glynnie. Not in Grinberry Falls."

"I know he's your husband's friend, but he and I are done. If I run into him, I'll simply ignore him."

"You're going to ignore Rhett Wilding? Yeah, I'm sure that'll work."

"There was a time when I couldn't have ignored him. But that time has passed."

"Okay. What are you doing tomorrow?"

"I'm meeting the painters here at ten. Once I confirm the paint is the right color, I'm coming to ask your husband for a favor."

"Anything I can help with?"

"My chandelier and settee are still at Rhett's. I'm not ready for the settee, but I need to clean the chandelier and get it ready to hang. I was wondering if Mav would be willing to pick it up for me."

"I'll mention it to him tonight. You know he will. Do you want some help cleaning and polishing? We could do it on our deck."

"If I say yes, will you ask Mav not to tell Rhett that I'm going to be there? Please don't set me up for an ambush, Brina."

"Hey, I would never do that to you. We'll put down a tarp, and you and I will be on chandelier scrubbing duty for as long as it takes. No boys allowed."

"Okay. Yeah, I could use some help. And company."

"She wants to be in the presence of another human. Progress!"

I laugh. "I'm sorry. I didn't mean to shut you out. I just—"

"Needed some space. I know. Welcome back."

"Thanks. I'm getting there."

***

The painters are ten minutes late, which logically I know is not a big deal, but I am keyed up and antsy and I really, really want to make it a big deal. Even after they apologize, I still want to spin out about it because it feels inadequate. Too little emotion. Not heartfelt enough.

But I say it's fine because when I take a moment to breathe before I unleash, I realize I don't trust myself to judge anyone's sincerity right now. Clearly, I'm not the great judge of character I thought I was.

Sabrina shows up as they're doing prep work, which is taking forever. I just need to see some paint on a wall. She's brought coffee and breakfast tacos, so we sit in her car and eat while listening to music. It gets us out of the painters' way and gets me out of my head.

She always knows what I need. I shouldn't have shut her out, not even for a little while, but sometimes, I don't have a huge amount of choice when it comes to withdrawing for a bit.

I always snap out of it, and thankfully, she's one of those intuitive types who will kick your emotional ass when needed but also give you space without holding a grudge.

Finally, one of the painters comes outside and says they're ready for me to come approve the paint color. Yes!

It's stunningly perfect. I'd prepared myself to be open to a slight variance from what I've had in my mind, but it's an exact match.

I feel like we're really in the home stretch now. I know from experience that once all the walls are painted the rest happens so fast.

The next few weeks will feel like everything is happening in triple time, and after so much waiting around for things to happen, I'm ready for it.

I don't have a signature wall color that's consistent in my locations because I want each one to fit where it is—from the building to the city to the vibe of the community. Each store has its own personality.

This swath of bright blue in front of me makes me happy. It's bold and vibrant. Everything I need this store to be. This one will be a little more eclectic than the others, which fits in an ever-changing place like Grinberry Falls, whether the locals know it yet or not.

Sugar Lips fits here.

The back door opens and it registers in my mind, but I don't jump. The painters have been going in and out all morning.

"Do you have a minute to talk?" His voice still generates a familiar comfort in me. And I hate him for it.

I don't answer him, just quietly seethe as I stare at my beautiful bright blue on the wall and imagine how gorgeously it will complement the wallpaper I've chosen.

"Just give me ten minutes," Rhett says. "Please."

How much longer is he going to stand there and be ignored?

"Talk to me, Twister!"

"Get out! Oh, lookie there, words coming right out of my mouth, commonly known as talking. I've talked. I'm done."

He closes his eyes and takes a deep breath. I brace myself for him to dig in and refuse to leave, but he opens his eyes and nods his head.

"When you're ready for the couch, I'll help Mav bring it over."

"No need. I'll hire someone."

He leaves without another word. Finally.

Enzo crosses paths with him on his way in. They exchange hellos, and I immediately want to forbid my general contractor from talking to him.

Instead, I smile at the painters and say, "It looks great, guys. Go for it."

This makes Enzo smile. "I love a day that starts good for everybody."

"Yeah, me, too."

But I'd like one to stay good the whole way through again at some point.

Mav's back at the house with my chandelier already set out on their back deck.

Sabrina rips into him as soon as we walk in. "You promised you wouldn't tell him where she was going to be! He walked in there like he knew for a fact she'd be there. His eyes weren't searching. He knew!"

"Wasn't her car there?"

"Don't be cute. You promised, Mav."

"No. I promised not to tell him she was coming over here to polish that chandelier. I never said a word about not telling him she was meeting with painters this morning."

"Why would you do that?"

"Because he's my friend and he's upset and they're good together and she just needs to talk to him so they can work this shit out and get back together."

I laugh at the absurdity of how simple he makes it sound. Like we're a couple of preschoolers who've had a fight on the playground. Men.

"Stay out of it, Mav," Sabrina warns. "If I can't interfere, you damn sure can't!"

Ah, so she agrees with him, but she's doing a better job of keeping her opinion to herself. Works for me.

I scrub every curve and angle of the brass flowers with a toothbrush, and then I polish until my hand cramps. Sabrina cleans the crystals with more care and precision than anyone else would. She's the only person I trust to help me do this. After she cleans each one, she rewraps it in fresh bubble wrap.

We are more alike than we are different. She knows how I want it done because it's exactly how she'd want it done.

"I need a break," I say.

"A water and hand stretching break, or a wine and charcuterie break?"

"Well, now that I know wine and charcuterie is an option . . ."

I slump into a chair at her kitchen table. I'm tired, and I know it's not just physical, but I don't have time for any of it.

"I'm really sorry Mav opened his big mouth and told Rhett you were going to be there this morning."

"Rhett could've just as easily shown up without the intel. I don't know if you've ever noticed, but he's not known for letting the lack of an invitation keep him away from anywhere he wants to be."

"This is true." She dumps cheese cubes onto a platter and turns to the sink to wash grapes. "Which probably means you should expect him to show up again, because he really, really wants to be with you."

"I heard wine. Is there not wine?"

"Mav just restocked the wine fridge. Take your pick."

"It's hard to stay mad at a guy with a wine fridge."

"Perks of marrying a bartender."

"He bought this thing for you, and you know it. Um, are these chocolate truffles in here also up for grabs?"

"That's where he put them! Merilee made them. I tore the fridge apart early searching for those. Yes, please. Bring the truffles."

Mav walks through and laughs at our break snacks.

"Thanks for the wine and chocolate," I say.

"You're welcome. How many glasses of that wine would it take for you to be willing to talk to Rhett?"

"I can only have one because I'm not done cleaning the chandelier yet. And later, when it's all done, if I decide to drink more wine, I will be tired and sore, and probably very cranky, so I'm going to let you do that math."

"Maybe another day."

"Or not. But I didn't get out of bed this morning to be a dream crusher, so you hold out hope wherever you need to."

I pop another dark-chocolate, raspberry, and whipped honey truffle into my mouth because they are quite possibly the best damn things I have ever tasted. And it's hard to say mean things with a mouth full of chocolate.

32

Rhett

THE STUDIO IS BOOKED all weekend, and I'm working in the booth. These musicians are old friends of mine. Familiarity makes the work easy. I could almost do this in my sleep, if I were sleeping as long as these sessions, which I'm not.

I saw a woman unloading wallpaper from a minivan in front of Sugar Lips this morning. Mav says she's set an official opening date. Two weeks.

He hung the chandelier for her yesterday. I was supposed to do that. I was there when she bought it, sat in that dusty barn and helped her make sure every crystal was there. Watched her eyes light up. Listened to her sneeze.

I punch in to put my voice in the singer's headphones. "Emotion's coming through strong, Aaron, but you came in a little late on that verse. Let's do it again for safety."

I'm not sure if he was really late or if I zoned out for a few seconds, but it won't hurt to retake. Better to give it a second shot while he's still in the flow than later.

Everybody sticks around for dinner. I fire up the grill and pass out beers. Bo begs way too effectively, and these guys are all suckers, feeding him bites of chicken every time I turn around. He'll go to bed happy tonight.

Lucky dog.

Before that happens, I agree to come to Nashville next week to catch their next show. Derringer's on tour right now, and he'll be playing while I'm there, too. It'll be good to get out of town and catch up with people I don't get to see much anymore, enjoy some live music.

NEVER LET IT BE said Derringer Wells has forgotten who helped him on his way up. He's playing an unannounced show at a smaller, but increasingly popular venue in Nashville tonight before his arena show tomorrow. It's one of the places that gave him a shot early on, back when they were as new as he was.

I walk to the green room to say hello and hang out until he goes on stage. Derringer is in his usual entertaining form, telling a story and using his hands as much as his mouth. It's a familiar sight.

But the woman sitting on his lap shocks the hell out of me. She's familiar, too, just not in this context.

"What are you doing here?" she and I ask each other at the same time.

Derringer laughs. "He does this," he tells her. "Pops up with no warning."

"I had no idea," she says.

Mav is going to lose his shit when he finds out about this. But I was right.

Derringer and Merilee look good together. I should've guessed this was going on. It's not like Derringer made a secret of his intentions. Mav will adjust.

"Well, at least I have somebody to sit with during the show," I say.

"I'll have them add you to the table," Derringer says. "You know everybody else who'll be sitting there, anyway."

"I already secured my seat, just didn't expect Merilee to be sitting with us."

"Of course you have. I don't know why I thought you'd need me to handle that."

"You like to think you're pretty important these days."

"I am," he says. "But you never miss an opportunity to let me know you've been around longer and know more people."

"Damn straight, kid."

He laughs again when I call him a kid. He knows good and well I'm a fan, no matter how much shit I give him.

There is no chance paparazzi won't get a picture of Merilee with him tonight. I may not have to break the news to Mav after all. I just hope she's ready for everything that comes with dating a famous musician. She's a small-town girl.

Her world is about to experience some big changes, not all of them pleasant, but he's from a small town, too. I assume he's prepared her. Or tried to, anyway.

Life changes on a dime sometimes.

33

Glynnis

T HREE DAYS UNTIL THE grand opening. Tonight's the private pre-opening reception. Staff is hired and they'll be working their first shifts, although it will be super informal. I've made sure they know I want them to enjoy the party, too.

It's a good chance for people, including me, to get to know them. But I feel good about the hiring choices I made.

Sabrina helped us fill the swag bags. The last time she and I put gift bags together was for her wedding. She gave me much less grief about these.

I've invited every woman I know in Grinberry Falls, all the shop owners on Main Street, and the owner of the coffee shop where Rhett and I crashed and burned.

I still feel awful about making a scene and disrupting everyone else who just trying to enjoy their evening. She's assured me that's not the worst outburst she's ever witnessed.

She won't see another display like that from me. Never again will I lose it like that in public.

I even invited Shayna Gibson to the reception, and told her to bring friends. I'm looking to make as many impressions as possible tonight. And I can't lie, I'm curious about what's happening with her and Landon since I paved the way for them to get reacquainted.

Joni and Sabrina show up early. I hadn't realized how anxious I was until I feel myself relax when they walk in. It's amazing how quickly a friendly face can settle your nerves.

"I'm glad you're finally done hogging all my general contractor's time," Joni teases.

She hired Enzo a few days ago to handle her remodel. I knew she'd like him. "He's all yours. Good luck with this town's archaic permitting process."

Sabrina holds out a gift bag. "Congratulations."

"Thank you."

She's stuffed a ridiculous amount of sparkly gold tissue paper into the bag, but when I remove the last of it, I shriek at what I find underneath.

"I love it!" I pull the vintage beaded purse up by its delicate chain. "You remembered my idea."

"Of course, I remembered."

I've been too preoccupied to find a purse for my planned under-the-counter display. So, she did it for me.

I open the glass cabinet and lay the purse open on the shelf, spreading the chain out in a way that looks like it could've fallen there. And then I fan out lipsticks as though they've spilled from it.

It's cute, but it needs something between all the gold lipstick tubes. Some color.

There are a few colorful things in the office . . . in my desk drawer where I've hidden them away because I wasn't sure I could bring myself to use them. Fuck it. It's time to end the pity party.

I stare at the swans on the cigarette case and the curlicues etched into the silver compact. It looks complete now, exactly the way I envisioned it.

May as well bring out the damn red phone, too.

It's the final touch this shelf needed, looking perfectly at home with the framed postcard. I lift the receiver, put my finger in the dial, and spin it. When I release it, my fingers gently twirl the cord being careful not to stretch the coils. If customers ruin this cord, I'm going to be livid.

Maybe I should put this under the counter as well. I step back and admire it sitting between my signature red collection with the cord dangling over the shelf's edge, and I know there's no way I'm putting that phone out of reach.

I'm sure I can get a replacement cord if I need one. This phone was meant to be touched. To bring people together.

"Hey, how are you doing?" Sabrina asks, resting her hand on my shoulder. "The real answer, not the tough-girl front."

"Not great. I'm super happy to be this close to opening, but I still miss him every day, and then I get mad at myself for being so weak and pathetic. It's just going to take more time."

Joni gives me a sympathetic smile, which is not an expression she's known for. I got to know her better during the week I spent hiding in her garage apartment. I'm back in Sabrina and Mav's cottage, but I consider Joni a friend now, too.

"Missing him doesn't make you weak," she says. "You might even want to give him a call at some point. And that wouldn't make you weak either. Hell, if you two worked things out, nobody would think it was because you're weak, Glynnis."

"I've got too much going on to try to fix a broken relationship. I'm too old to be doing that shit, anyway."

"Oh, right. I forgot there was an age limit on that."

Her sarcasm comes through loud and clear, and weirdly, I appreciate it. Joni only talks like that to people she likes. But I try extra hard not to talk about Rhett with her. She was his friend first, and I don't want to put her in an awkward position.

He doesn't open up to a lot of people, but I think she might be one of the ones he feels comfortable enough to confide in. Everybody needs their people.

Most days I wish I'd never met him, but I don't hate him. I just don't want a man who can't be in my corner when other people are around. If we're only good in private, we're not good enough.

He showed me his limitations, and I've never been a big fan of limits in general.

Love me out loud or get the fuck out.

"Okay," I say. "Let's turn on the sign."

"Let me get my phone," Sabrina says. "We need video."

She and Joni run out to the sidewalk with their phones poised to capture the first lighting of the neon pink lips. I flip the switch, and they cheer like the ball just dropped on New Year's Eve.

They dance and spin in the strobe of flashing lips, and I can't imagine anything that could make me happier. I don't bother getting my own phone. The inaugural lighting is captured in video, and Sabrina will take a still shot of the sign from every angle.

I'll have enough content for weeks-worth of social media posts by the time she's done tonight.

Shayna Gibson arrives, carrying a bottle of champagne in each hand and leading an entourage. Looks like she invited every woman she knows in Grinberry Falls, too.

Joni and Sabrina follow them in, exchanging baffled expressions over this parade of women.

"Wow," I say. "You definitely spread the word."

"Is that okay? You said to bring people."

"It's great. The more, the merrier."

"Good." Her hands jut forward, presenting the bottles of bubbly. "These are for you."

"Thanks, but you didn't have to do that."

"Well, I have something to celebrate, too. And I owe it to you."

"You and Landon have talked?"

"We've done more than talk."

All her friends crack up. Based on the way they hoot and holler for her, I'd say they've done a little pregaming. Fine by me. The more smiling faces in the photos, the better.

Sabrina's mouth hangs open for a moment at Shayna's reveal.

When she recovers, she smiles at me and says, "I guess you managed to play matchmaker after all."

"You of all people should know better than to doubt me."

My staff arrives together, and I leave the women to pop their corks and browse. Sabrina hands out plastic champagne flutes while I go over last-minute details with my new employees.

In no time, the store is brimming with women, sipping champagne in between trying our lipstick and glosses. Their questions are being answered, glasses are being filled, and plates piled with charcuterie and sweet treats.

Women continue to stream in.

The chatty trio on the settee try the lip mask samples from the bowl on the side table. A couple of older women pass the red phone's receiver back and forth, giggling as if they're reliving something.

I built it, and they came.

Sugar Lips is full, and so is my heart.

But my eyes keep drifting to the door. It's a habit, one I know I need to break, but I look for him, expect him, at some point every day, no matter where I am.

He won't come here. He wouldn't dare. Not to something so stupid and pointless. And I don't want him here either. It's just a bad habit.

It'll break with time.

Merilee shoves a lip scrub tester under Joni's nose, and they both nod. I walk over to see which one they're giving their stamp of approval.

"Why do you recommend using a brush to apply darker shades of lipstick?" Joni asks.

"It's more precise, and you can really define the Cupid's bow." I take a clean brush and outline my lips in red, and then I paint inside the lines I've created.

"Oh, okay. That makes sense."

I reach for a tissue to blot the excess lip color I've applied for the demonstration, but before I can bring it to my lips, the door opens again.

Dropping the tissue on the counter, I pick up some samples and turn, eager to welcome more guests.

But I can save my samples.

Fuck me, I manifested him!

That shit finally worked—the universe tuned in—for this? Not for quicker permits or a deal on a billboard or more conveniently scheduled yoga classes . . .

No, the universe sends me the last damn thing I need tonight.

"I don't mean to break up the party," he says. "Just wanted to bring you this while I was down here."

When I get within arm's reach of him, he holds out a small, wooden bird. A chickadee?

The sudden silence around us is deafening. I cannot afford to come undone in front of these women. This is my introduction to most of them, and screaming obscenities isn't great for building a customer base.

I relax my shoulders and soften my jaw until I'm reasonably sure I don't look like an attack dog jonesing to sink my teeth into an intruder's jugular.

"Where did that come from?" I ask, hoping no one else recognizes the animosity trembling in my voice.

There's no way I can look anywhere but directly at him. If I look around and see people staring at us, watching us, waiting for me to snap, I just might.

"Found it under a bed." His smile is subtle, barely perceptible.

I tell myself it's a smirk, but even I can't deny that it's too openly vulnerable to qualify. There is not a whiff of arrogance about him, and it unmoors me. I grapple for anything that will anchor me to my convictions. Anger, disgust . . . any solid emotion with no soft spots will do.

"At your house?" I ask as the realization sinks like a rock in my stomach. "So, this was one of your grandmother's birds? I can't take that. I'm sure someone in your family would probably like to have it, though."

His beard is trimmed to the length I like. And, of course, he's shown up in pearl snaps.

"No one in my family wants this bird. It's okay if you don't either. I just wanted to offer it to you before I got rid of it. You said before that you would've wanted one."

This is a conniving attempt to exploit my sentimental side—a side I never should've shown him—and I'm not falling for it.

"You should keep it."

"Why? So I can think of you every time I look at it? Because that's all it's ever going to do for me."

"It's adorable. I'm sure it won't sit in the thrift shop for long." I walk away from him.

"Glynnis Alexandria Ramsey, stop!"

I want to kick my own ass when my feet obey his command. I start walking again.

"Red light!"

He thinks using my safe words is going to work for him? When he's the one I need to be kept safe from?

"I miss you," he says to my back. And then he raises his voice. "I miss you because I love you."

My inner voice screams at me to ignore him, but my body refuses to listen. I spin with enough speed and fury to justify his nickname for me.

"Yeah, I can't tell you how loved I felt hearing you belittle me in front of your friends. Listening to you be such a cool guy, laughing at me and—"

"If you'd stayed in your chair for another thirty seconds instead of flying off the goddamn handle, you'd have heard me go on to tell them that it doesn't matter if your business is a passing fad, because you'll come up with something new. You'll pivot. You'll survive it because that's what you do. You're a brilliant, beautiful survivor, Twister. I've always known that. I love you and I respect you, and I'm sorry that you heard me say something hurtful, but I promise you I wasn't done talking."

"You about done now?"

"Is that what you want? For this to be done?"

"It already is."

His steps are calm as he walks away. No angry posture or words. No slamming door behind him.

The moment the door closes, my eyes find Sabrina. I desperately search her gaze for support, solidarity, sisterhood, anything to extinguish the hot tears I'm fighting to hold back . . . but all I find is disappointment written all over her face.

My eyes flit away from hers to meet with Joni's.

"Glynnis, I've known that man for a long time. There is not another woman in the world he would've done that for."

Nope. Not looking to hear that right now. I find Merilee because I don't need romanticized notions. I need grit.

"I swear, Glynnis, if you don't go after him right now, I will. And I'll tell him you sent me to bring him back, and if that doesn't work, I'll drag him back in here, even if I have to knee him in the balls and stick a finger in his eye to get it done."

"You're all a bunch of traitors! Dammit. Do you know how much I hate it when people meddle in other people's personal lives?"

They laugh, and the irony is not lost on me. But when I play matchmaker, I do it because I truly believe those two people might be good for each other.

I look around at all these caring faces, and the smolder in the pit of my stomach flares to an inferno.

I burst through the door onto the sidewalk.

"Rhett Everett Wilding, stop!"

His steps halt, and he turns to hear what I'll say next.

That actually worked? Shit, what do I say next? My thoughts are too scrambled to make sense, and my pulse is throbbing so loud I can't hear myself think.

My shoulders lift as I blink back tears. "Green light?"

Shaking his head, he walks toward me.

"I swear, you are impossible to deal with sometimes."

"Yeah, well, sometimes, you're an asshole."

He throws his arms up. "Not on purpose!"

"Gimme that bird!"

His pulls me close and stares into my eyes. "Don't ever walk away from me without giving me a chance to explain myself again."

"Give. Me. That. Bird."

My fingers close around the precious heirloom. How could I not smile with this little, round chickadee in my hand? "Thank you."

"You're welcome. Did you come after me just for the bird?"

"Mostly. But I also needed to say I love you, and I'm sorry, too."

"Coming in second to a wooden bird is probably not the worst position I've ever been in."

"You don't come second, Rhett. That's why it hurt so much."

"I know. And I'm truly sorry."

"I believe you. But I kind of need to get back to my party you interrupted."

"I'll be at Grin's when it's over."

"I hear Derringer's playing tonight."

"Not that I'm aware of," he says.

"Maybe you don't know as much as you think you do."

"Is that right? How would you happen to know he's playing tonight?"

"Let's just say a little birdie told me."

"Is this little birdie a nurse who waits tables part-time?"

"Show off."

"See you at Grin's, Twister."

"See you there, Daddy."

He pops a couple of snaps just to torment me.

I'd flash him if I wasn't worried about someone jumping around the corner with a camera. If the press knows Derringer is expected to be at Grin's tonight, it's highly possible. His latest release is sitting at number one.

Damn, it sucks being a responsible adult.

The neon lips bathing our shadows in pink light remind me why it's worth it. But his pearl snaps shining under the streetlamp are more temptation than I can deny.

I pull him along my narrow driveway between Sugar Lips and the boutique next door until we're well out of the glow of the streetlamp before I flash him. It's not as spontaneous as I'd have liked, but it's effective.

He groans and steps closer as I yank my shirt down and take a step back.

"You can look, but you can't touch. Not yet. See you at the bar."

"We won't be there long."

"We'll have to stick around for Derringer's show."

"No, we're going home for a private show."

"Cool," I say. "I can't wait to see your act."

"Oh, I'll perform for you."

He pushes me against the side of my little blue house and kisses me, touching wherever he wants. I push him away gently, pop a few more of his snaps, and plant my lips on his chest, leaving a red kiss print, and then I re-snap his shirt, hiding it away from the world.

"Looking forward to it," I say with a teasing smile.

"We can go right now."

"We absolutely cannot. Have my martini ready and waiting for me."

"Shoot me a text when your party's wrapping up. Plan on drinking it quickly."

The whole reception breaks into applause when I walk back into Sugar Lips.

Sabrina offers me a champagne flute as she says, "Here's to the men we love."

I take the glass and lift it to hers. "Here's to the men who love us."

"And if the men we love don't love us?"

"Then fuck them, and here's to us!" I finish the toast.

Everyone cheers.

I laugh and take a sip. "Whatever happened to those wild girls who used to make that toast every night?"

Sabrina shrugs. "I heard they grew up and fell in love with a couple of small-town guys."

"Huh," I say. "That's sounds about like some stupid shit they would've done."

"I guess they always were a little softer than they wanted to admit."

"No, they were badasses."

"Fuck yeah, we were. Your shirt's a little twisted, by the way."

DERRINGER IS ALREADY ON stage when we walk into Grin's. Rhett is sitting on a barstool talking to Mav behind the bar. He hasn't seen me yet. I take a moment to watch him, remembering the first time I laid eyes on him, right here in this bar. Derringer was on stage that night, too.

It feels like a reset button has been pressed, and we get to start over.

He sees me now. And I know beyond the shadow of a doubt that we can't start fresh. We have too much history. Memories I wouldn't erase if I could. Most of them, anyway. But that's what happens when you let some arrogant man trick you into falling in love with him.

His beard is the perfect length. His smile is sexy as hell. And those pearl snaps are calling my name.

I sit on the barstool next to his.

"I thought you'd never get here," he says, sliding an espresso martini toward me.

"The reception went better than I could've hoped. It's been a good night, all things considered."

"Night's not over yet."

"That sounds like a threat." I take a gulp of my martini so it doesn't go entirely to waste. "You about ready to get out of here and make good on it?"

"I'm always ready for you, Twister."

"You were so unprepared for me when we met."

"No. I'd been waiting my whole damn life for you.

34

Glynnis

ONE YEAR LATER

RHETT TURNS THE KEY in the lock and pushes the door open. "Damn, that paint smell is still strong. We need to open some windows."

"Remember how surprised you were the last time I bought a house?" I walk past him and set the peace lily our realtor gave me at closing in the entryway.

"*You* didn't buy this one. *We* did."

"It looks so much bigger with no furniture in it."

"It is big."

He's not wrong, but he's also the one who fell head-over-heels for this place within five minutes. He was tired of staying in my small condo when we're in Arizona, so we decided to buy a house outside of Scottsdale where the traffic is lighter.

I open the living room windows. We can't see our closest neighbor from this room, just cactus, rocks, and chipmunks during the daylight. The after-dark wildlife will probably take some getting used to—for me, at least. Rhett grew up listening to coyotes howling and seeing bobcat tracks. And occasionally, bigger cat tracks.

I'm not looking forward to either one, but we have acreage, so I know it comes with the territory. When I say we're outside of town, we are way outside. The man loves wide open spaces.

And we both love this big house.

He's already talked to a contractor about converting the largest guest bedroom into a recording studio. Now that we've officially taken possession, we can sign the contract and get that project started.

We'll need all these extra rooms and entertaining space for the musicians he'll no doubt invite to stay with us while they record or when they pass through on tour.

His studio here won't have the same legendary reputation, but we're back in Grinberry Falls often enough to accommodate the artists who can't get past their superstition about recording in his original studio.

"We've got a lot of furniture shopping to do," I say.

"All we need today is a bed."

"That will be here in . . ." I glance at the time on my phone. "About forty minutes, according to the driver's last text."

"Take off your pants."

"No. But if you can catch me, you can take them off."

I run for the hallway, forgetting the dining room also connects to it. He takes the shortcut and blocks my path, but I break free.

"You can't run again after I catch you!"

"What? I can't hear you from so far away."

I turn into the primary bedroom and hide behind the door. He walks in with no urgency, so certain he's found me.

He checks the closet, and then he moves on to the attached bathroom.

As soon as he crosses the threshold into the bathroom, I slip from my current hiding spot into the closet he's already searched and quietly pull the door closed behind me.

Hide-and-seek was always my best game. It's made for quick thinkers with light steps. The best strategy is always to keep moving, darting from one hiding spot to another. Quick, light steps, fast as fast can be.

I bite my lip in the dark, reveling in the satisfaction of tricking him.

The door flies open, and I squeal. "Dammit! How'd you know?"

"You can't hide from me."

I step forward to exit the large, windowless closet, but he advances and recloses the door, trapping us both in the cool dark space.

"Take everything off."

I strip naked, dropping my clothes to the floor around me, unable to see my own hand in front of my face. "All done, Daddy."

My body is aware of him being close, but I quiver in anticipation of his touch. I can't predict which direction it will come from, and the uncertainty of the space between us sends a surge of adrenaline through me.

He holds stock still just to antagonize me, to challenge my comfort and heighten the element of surprise when his hands finally reach for me.

I back up a few paces, unaware if he's moving or not until his palms land with smooth accuracy on my sides just above my hips—no fumbling at all.

It's as if he could see me, but there's no way. The light isn't on in the bedroom, and the blinds are closed. There's no glow seeping under the door to cast shadows.

"How did you touch me so easily when you can't even see me?"

"I don't need light to see you."

My nipples seize when his thumbs graze over them. He pinches, and my core clenches. His hands glide to my back, and he pulls me closer so he can kiss me. There is no near-miss with his lips. And when his mouth moves down my neck and chest, it has no problem finding my nipples he's plumped.

He sucks hard, and I can see him in my mind's eye, but when I attempt to look down at him, he is invisible. Surely, my eyes should be adjusting by now, but I have to blink to determine if they're open or closed.

"Turn around and put your hands on the wall," he says in his lurid, raspy voice, the one that usually makes his commands impossible for me not to obey.

But I can't comply this time without reservation. "You can't see me. You might strike my back instead or—"

"My hand will have no problem finding your gorgeous ass in the dark. Trust me. Turn around and put your hands on the wall."

I have to grope for the wall, so I don't actually trust that he'll be able to spank me where he intends, but my hands press firmly for support.

His warm hand touches me gently, following the curve of my ass, pausing to knead my flesh. He groans, and I love the way the raw sound surrounds us.

And then his hand leaves my skin for the few seconds it takes him to lift it high enough to slap hard when he brings it back down—exactly where he'd been squeezing.

I moan as the sting builds between strikes. My eyes finally begin to adjust, showing me the solidness of my forearms in contrast with the emptiness around them.

"Turn around and press your back against the wall."

I'm not ready for him to stop yet, but we don't have the luxury of time, and I don't want to be naked in a closet when the delivery truck arrives.

The sound of his belt being unbuckled and falling slack sends goosebumps up my arms. When the metal teeth of his zipper separate to open the front of his pants, a shiver racks my spine.

He lifts my leg, but when I try to wrap it around his waist, he forces it still in mid-air. And then he drops to his knees and brings my foot to rest on his shoulder. My vision has increased enough to distinguish his form, but I still feel clumsy in the face of his dauntless choreography.

Once he's on his knees, his head is too far away for me to see it, but I swear I can feel his hot mouth on my pussy seconds before it actually makes contact. His beard is soft against my tender skin, but the scrape of his teeth is savage as his tongue furiously probes and licks.

My fingers curl into his hair, poised to rip it out of his scalp if he slows or lessens his force.

I scream loud enough to fill every empty void in the house when his efforts pay off. We don't even have a towel for his face, but he doesn't sound fazed by the flood when he commands me to resume my hands-on-the-wall position.

His dick is so thick and hard I can't keep my heels on the ground as he slams it into me. My toes lift another inch, but there is no reprieve from his quickening thrusts. His strong fingers dig into my hips, and the powerful grip may be the only thing keeping me upright.

I'm positive the moment he lets go of me I'm going to collapse at his feet.

He holds on tightly through the waves of his release, only letting his fingers relax after the last jolt of his hips forces the final grunt from his lungs.

My legs are still shaking when the doorbell chime echoes from the speaker in the hallway.

Shit! There's no way we've been in here for forty minutes.

Rhett zips his jeans and buckles his belt.

"I can't find my clothes." We've traveled farther into the closet since I shed them.

He opens the door enough to create shadows, but before I can get to dark heaps on the floor that identify my clothes, he bends down and retrieves them for me.

"I've got it," he says.

I pause to let him pick them up, which he does.

And then he rushes out of the closet with them, closing me in the darkness again.

"Rhett, get back here!" I bolt from the closet to follow him, but by the time I step into the hall, he's rounded into the living room.

I run back to our bedroom, past the open closet and into the bathroom, locking the door behind me to wait out the assembly of our new bed—by strange men separated from my naked body by nothing more than a hollow door.

All the rooms in this house, and I ran back into this one?

Oh, he'll pay for this.

He. Will. Pay.

I sit on the toilet with my legs crossed, silently plotting terrible retribution as I listen to Rhett's friendly banter on the other side of the door.

My bladder sends me another reminder that it needs to be emptied, but there is no way I'm going to pee for them to hear and wonder who he's holding captive in the bathroom.

It's bad enough they're here; I don't need them sending the cops in for a wellness check after they leave.

I can just see the smug smile on Rhett's face, the smile that I'm going to slap off of him as soon as I can leave this room.

Finally, I hear verbal exchanges that indicate the job's all done. As soon as their voices fade down the hallway, I pee. The sweet relief of it nearly brings tears to my eyes.

I wait until I hear the truck driving away before I come out of the bathroom.

"You asshole!" I yell as I storm down the hall in search of him.

He greets me with the arrogant smile I'd already envisioned when I find him in the kitchen. My clothes are folded neatly on the kitchen island . . . next to a bottle of champagne.

"Who brought champagne?"

"I did. I was hoping we might want to celebrate."

"All I want to do right now is knock that smirk off your face."

"Can you give me a minute before you swing? I'm not sure I'll be able to talk after you knock my mouth off."

I bite the inside of my lip to keep from smiling at his smart-ass reply.

He backs me into the counter and drops to his knees.

"Oh, no, that won't get you out of this."

Before I can push him away, he unclasps his raised hand to reveal a small, blue leather box resting on his palm. Is he really . . .

He opens the hinged lid, and the double-framed, emerald-cut diamond nestled in the pillowy satin steals my breath.

"You couldn't let me put my clothes on before you did this?"

"The only thing I want to see you wearing right now is this ring."

"Well, then I guess you better put it on my finger."

His hand shakes a little as he gently pushes the Art Deco setting past my knuckle.

Now, my hand is shaking. This is the most beautiful ring I've ever seen.

"What do you think about marrying a smirky asshole who loves you more than the air he breathes?"

"I think a girl could do worse."

"That's a yes, right?"

"That's a hell yes, Daddy."

His soft kiss makes my legs weak all over again.

The cork releases on a quiet sigh, no loud pop.

"It's good luck when it opens quietly like that," I say.

He smiles. "Is that right?"

We pass the bottle back and forth because we haven't even brought in glasses. This feels more like us, anyway.

"I guess I'll get dressed again at some point before the wedding," I say, handing the bottle back to him.

"Shhh, you're not supposed to say mean things during a celebration."

Our laughter fills the room. And then he pours champagne over my chest. What he can't catch with his tongue runs to the floor, christening our kitchen with its first sticky mess.

Which also feels a lot like us. We make messes. It's kind of our thing.

And then we survive them.

Thank you so much for reading Glynnis and Rhett's story. I hope you enjoyed your introduction to the Grinberry Falls series and are looking forward to rest of the love stories that will unfold there soon.

If you would like to leave an online review, it will be immensely appreciated!

AND . . .

If you missed Glynnis and Rhett's initial meeting, you can find it in the final novella from the Rocky Start Romance novella series, Chased Shot. You can see them again in the Christmas novella, Just for Grin's.

Book 2, If You Like It, I Love It, is coming your way early summer 2026. This is Joni and Enzo's story. After all the love Joni shows her beloved alpaca, Oliver, and her friends in Grinberry Falls, it's her turn to be showered with attention. And a younger man may be just what she needs in her life. Enzo is more than just a general contractor, y'all.

Book 3, Don't Let the Doorknob Hit You, will be released in fall 2026. This is Merilee and Derringer's story. If you met Derringer all the way back in Missed Exit, you've seen him come a long way. Merilee deserves the world, and he's determined to give it to her, even if they have to fake a breakup to have a moment's peace.

Please visit my website at https://indiesparks.net to subscribe to my newsletter to stay updated about releases and signing events plus exclusive content!

You can find me on social media as well:
Instagram and Facebook as "Indie Sparks Author"
You are always welcome in my Facebook Readers Group: "Fast
Burns and Happy Turns – Indie Sparks Readers Group"